PLAYING WITH FIRE

Lord Edward seized Emily by the shoulders and he drew her up against his chest as his mouth swooped down to cover hers. He pressed his lips against hers passionately, his wide-open green eyes staring unblinkingly into her wide-open brown ones, in order to gauge her reaction. He slanted his mouth first one way, then the other, without ever breaking contact, employing all of his considerable romantic skill, while his hands left her shoulders to press her against him from knee to breast.

Emily thought it would be child's play to lead the handsome, charming and supremely self-confident Lord Edward Laurence on a fool's chase of love. But she forgot one thing. She was not a child—she was a woman. . . .

MICHELLE KASEY is the pseudonym of Kasey Michaels, which is the pseudonym of Kathie Seidick, a suburban Pennsylvania native who is also a full-time wife and the mother of four children. Her love of romance, humor and history combines to make Regency novels her natural medium.

SIGNET REGENCY ROMANCE
COMING IN MARCH 1989

Ellen Fitzgerald
An Unwelcome Alliance

Carla Kelly
Summer Campaign

Emily Hendrickson
Hidden Inheritance

The Enterprising Lord Edward

Michelle Kasey

A SIGNET BOOK

NEW AMERICAN LIBRARY

PUBLISHED BY
PENGUIN BOOKS CANADA LIMITED

NAL BOOKS ARE AVAILABLE AT QUANTITY DISCOUNTS WHEN
USED TO PROMOTE PRODUCTS OR SERVICES. FOR INFORMATION
PLEASE WRITE TO PREMIUM MARKETING DIVISION, NEW AMERI-
CAN LIBRARY, 1633 BROADWAY, NEW YORK, NEW YORK 10019.

First Printing, February, 1989

2   3   4   5   6   7   8   9

Ⓞ SIGNET TRADEMARK REG. U.S. PAT OFF AND FOREIGN COUNTRIES
REGISTERED TRADEMARK — MARCA REGISTRADA
HECHO EN WINNIPEG, CANADA

SIGNET, SIGNET CLASSIC, MENTOR, ONYX, PLUME,
MERIDIAN and NAL BOOKS are published in Canada by Penguin
Books Canada Limited, 2801 John Street, Markham, Ontario,
Canada L3R 1B4
PRINTED IN CANADA
COVER PRINTED IN U.S.A.

To Congenial Eddie Charles and his lovely wife, Kay—otherwise known as my parents—on the occasion of their fiftieth wedding anniversary. I love ya, guys.

Prologue

"Yes, yes. I believe I like this new way you've found with my cravat. Very well, Burton, I think I'll do now, thank you. It's time for me to sally forth once again into the fray. She still hates me, you know. It's most lowering for a man like me, who's so used to females falling at his feet. And don't frown—I know I'm being immodest. It's part of my boyish charm. You don't suppose there's some other way to go about this?"

Burton looked up at the author of these self-serving statements as that man's upper body was reflected down to him in the dressing-stand mirror. As usual, his master was the epitome of sartorial perfection, although his servant would be the last ever to tell him that. "There's always incarceration, I imagine, my lord, if you've the stomach for it."

Lord Edward Laurence allowed his fine broad shoulders to slump forward dejectedly, momen-tarily destroying the fine line of his new evening coat. "You're always so subtle, Burton. Papa

7

should never have set you loose in his library, you little demon. 'Incarceration.' Oh, yes, indeed, that alternative would send my poor sire to spinning in his grave for sure. No, I've no real alternative, do I? But you could at least offer me some compassion, you know. I'm too young to be purposely contemplating coming to such a sad end, even if she is so superior a female."

"Yes, my lord," Burton answered quietly, unimpressed by this show of despair, for he knew it to be only that, and his master was more than ready to meet his fate. "If you've done with admiring yourself, shall I fetch your evening cloak?"

"You may, confound you. It isn't seemly, Burton, to appear always in so much of a rush. I'm sure Reggie can be left to his own devices for a few more weeks without all of Lyndhurst Hall coming to grief. Do you suppose I should let Monty have the writing of my epitaph? Something like 'Here lies Lord Edward; gone the way of Matrimony'?"

"Your father, rest his long-suffering soul, would be most proud of you, my lord," the servant said bolsteringly, clambering onto a nearby handy chair so that he could slip the burgundy satin evening cloak around his lordship's shoulders, adding, "although I doubt he'd have gone so far as to endorse your methods of ensuring the line."

Lord Edward grinned into the mirror, gifting his servant with a reflected wink. "We both agree

I must marry, little general, and soon, but I don't recall promising not to have myself a little fun along the way. Besides, the female I'm considering can't see me for dust, something she has brought home to me quite forcefully every time we meet. Dear me, do you suppose that's why I've chosen her? Perhaps I am insincere; perhaps I have not totally reconciled myself to my fate."

Burton sniffed derisively as he replaced the chair in a corner of the dressing room and tugged his waistcoat lower over his protruding stomach. "I still believe a more straightforward method to be best, as we are pressed for time."

Shaking his head in the negative, a movement that sent a single lock of dark blond hair tumbling back down onto his forehead, its favorite resting place, Lord Edward replied mischievously, "Too tame by half, Burton, old man, and too damned boring as well. Although I imagine I could fling a sack over her head and spirit her off to Gretna and have done with this intrigue. Be happy I'm only planning to make her aware of me for a start. Besides, I must still get her down to Lyndhurst to make sure she and Reggie will be compatible, before I actually allow myself to be led to the altar. Who knows, it may turn out that she is the wrong solution altogether. I couldn't be happy with her, no matter how well we might suit, if she couldn't be happy with Reggie."

"She's suitable," the little servant said, getting some small measure of his own back as he followed his master out onto the landing and down the stairs. "After all, she doesn't like you, does she?"

1

"Gad, Ned, but I love a farce!"

Lord Edward leaned back in the seat in his private box and drawled, "But, my dear Monty, much as I hate to see you cast down, I do believe the author's intent was quite serious."

Lord Henry Montgomery was immediately crestfallen, lowering his almost nonexistent chin onto his cravat and thrusting out his thin lower lip. "If you're correct, Ned, it means that I have vastly overestimated the man. I believed him to be *deliberately* awful."

"You must be shattered," Lord Edward observed mildly, his lips twitching as he delighted in his friend's chagrin. "However, the little warbler is rather nice, if a bit chicken-breasted. Or am I wrong, and you aren't harboring plans in her direction?"

"I am not!" Lord Henry, flushing, protested at once, before adding more softly, "Besides, Del's already stolen a march on me, blast him for a clumsy, overgrown Romeo. He's meeting her for a late supper, unless he's been telling tales, which wouldn't surprise me."

"Leaving the two of us to brave the Duchess of Chilworth's party alone." Lord Edward sighed deeply, as if resigning himself to the inevitable boredom of the evening, then added more hopefully, "One can only hope Lady Georgiana will still be free for a waltz. My heart is already pitter-pattering at the thought."

Lord Henry snorted derisively. "Hah! Your heart never pitter-pattered in your entire life. It beats most slowly and regularly all the time you are breaking female hearts throughout Mayfair— or at least it did the last time you were in town. So far this Season you have been almost dull. Time was you'd have given Del a real run for his money with that songbird. I gather it is Lady Georgiana's turn to crumple at your feet now that you're confining yourself to eligible young ladies. At least she'll do it gracefully—she's a remarkable dancer."

Leisurely rising from his seat, as the play had at last ground down to its uninspired conclusion, Lord Edward stood back to allow his friend to pass in front of him and out into the crowded corridor. "How you malign me, Monty, all because I have committed the grave sin of—at long last—growing up. Yes, you have found me out. It's true—I am on the lookout for a wife."

"Surely you jest!"

"Strange, is it not? Perhaps it has something to do with my advanced age. But only think about it a moment, Monty. I'll soon be celebrating my thirty-second, you know. With my dear brother Reginald already knocking at the door of fifty, and showing no signs of taking himself a wife, I really must consider setting up my own nursery. It is no more than my duty."

"You actually want me to think about Naughty Ned becoming serious about a female," Lord Henry mused, pursing his lips. "The mind reels. But surely not Lady Georgiana? That's taking sacrifice a step too far, if you ask me. But never say I didn't stand by you. Shall you be wishing for me to compose an ode to her vacant green eyes—not that she'll understand more than every third word of it."

They slowly made their way through the crush leading down the staircase to the street, the taller Lord Edward thoughtfully guiding his friend by the elbow as he spied out his carriage waiting a little way down the street. "Poetry is always nice," was all he said, remembering his earlier jest to Burton. "You don't approve of Lady Georgiana, Monty?"

"As a pretty ornament to be worn on your sleeve, perhaps, Ned. But as mother to these children you seem to be wanting? Hardly. She's totally lacking in wit. I read her my poem *Love's Splinter Smote My Eye*—you remember it, I'm sure, as you said it was one of your favorites—and all she had to say for herself when I was done was to blink those outrageous eyes at me and ask if I'd seen a physician about having the thing removed. I nearly wept, I tell you."

Lord Edward hid his amusement in a discreet cough, gave his driver directions to bear them to the duchess's residence in Portman Square, and then followed his friend into the carriage. "She may be deeper than you think, Monty," he pointed out helpfully, "and meant her words as a literary criticism. Had you thought of that?"

"Of course she did," Lord Henry responded waspishly. "Forgive me for doubting her. Lady Georgiana is deep. She's as deep as the Dead Sea. Now explain to me, if you can, her comment that Byron was being rather mean to have called his friend Boatswain a *dog* in the inscription on the fellow's own tombstone."

Now Lord Edward threw back his head and roared in utter delight. "She didn't! Did you explain to the poor dear that Boatswain *was*, after all, a Newfoundland?"

Lord Henry was laughing now too, for, he reasoned, if Lady Georgiana had insulted the great Byron as well, he was in good company. "I did," he said, barely able to control his voice for his mirth. "She said—and I swear, Ned, she did it with a straight face—she said it didn't matter one whit to her if the unfortunate fellow *was* a foreigner, Byron showed a sad lack of manners."

When he had recovered from his fit of hilarity, wiping his streaming eyes with the crisp white handkerchief he had pulled from his coat pocket, Lord Edward said, "Now I know she must have been hoaxing you. *Nobody* could be that obtuse. I will have to make a special point of standing up with her at least three times tonight."

Lord Henry sat stiffly in the far corner of the carriage, his beaky, pointed nose stuck high in the air, bracing himself against the inevitable jostling caused by the poor condition of London's streets and Lord Edward's driver's utter disregard for his passengers. "Old Horry will be *aux anges* when she hears it, I'm sure," he said archly, "—if she can remember your name."

2

"Old Horry"—known more formally as Hortense, Her Grace, the dowager Duchess of Chilworth—decided that she had spent sufficient time in playing the gracious hostess.

She had been standing at the head of the long curving stairs of the mansion for what must have been hours, greeting everyone and his wife, having her hand hurtfully wrung by beefy, overzealous fists, being poked in the eye by deadly ostrich plumes as papery powdered and scented cheeks were pressed against her own, being called upon to remember titles, and faces, and—worse yet—the names and dispositions of various faceless offspring that meant less than nothing to her but seemed of the utmost importance to the proud parents who mentioned them—all while standing on that hard marble floor in quite the most uncomfortable slippers it had ever been her misfortune to wear.

"They are rather lovely, though," she mused aloud, at last quitting her post and moving toward a chair she knew to be particularly kind to weary bones. "All silvery, and with the sweetest bows."

"I beg your pardon, Aunt Hortense?"

"Oh, it's you . . . um . . ."

"Emily, Aunt Hortense, your sister's eldest," Emily Howland supplied, trying not to sigh.

"M'sister's child? Which one would that be, dear?"

"Minerva, Aunt Hortense," Emily clarified. "She's the one with the large teeth," she added carefully, thus avoiding the next sure-to-be-asked question.

Emily had been in Portman Square for just above a month, the poor relation sent to companion her cousin Georgiana during the latter miss's come-out. But each time she approached her aunt she had to introduce herself as if for the first time. The woman was sweet, but she was becoming just a bit wearing. Surely nobody could be this vague—although her mother had warned her it was so.

"Just tell her about my teeth," Emily's mother had told her as she kissed her daughter goodbye in Surrey. "I once bit her arm badly when we were younger, and it seems to have left an indelible impression. Perhaps you might try it yourself, my dear, if all else fails."

"Of course . . . Emily. I knew that," the duchess said now, smiling up into her niece's face, for the girl was unusually tall. "You don't have her teeth, thank goodness, do you? What a horrid brat Minerva was, and it *was* my kitten, after all. But why are you standing here, child? Shouldn't you be with Georgy?"

"Georgiana's dancing, Aunt, and has been since the very first. She's had no end of partners, although I've been careful not to allow her more than two dances with any one gentleman, just as you told me. I thought I might offer you some refreshments."

Her grace lowered herself carefully into the chair, feeling more fragile this evening than usual. "How sweet. How thoughtful. How very . . . um . . . er . . ."

". . . considerate. Yes, of course, Aunt," Emily hastened to supply a suitable word when the duchess began to falter. "There's some lovely punch in the other room, if you'd care for a drink."

"Punch, Miss Howland? Nonsense! Only nectar of the gods will do for the dearest Duchess of Chilworth. Monty, be a good sport and fetch some for her grace at once!"

Emily's back stiffened angrily at the familiar-sounding voice and she turned to confront Lord Edward Laurence, disapproval evident in her set expression. The man was fast becoming the major bane of her existence. "You," she said flatly, refusing to lift her head so that she could look into his mocking eyes.

"*C'est moi*," Lord Edward agreed happily enough, only slightly inclining his head to acknowledge her rude greeting. "And how fares our resident dragon this evening? Have you found other employment as a serving wench, or has

Lady Georgiana at last managed to slip her leash? I had begun to fear the two of you were joined at the hip."

"Sirrah!"

"Now what?" he asked, frowning down at her bowed chestnut head. "Oh, I've been indelicate, haven't I? It's a failing of mine. Allow me to rephrase that. You were joined at the *hand*. There, never let it be said I was ignorant of your sensibilities."

"No, let's not," Emily muttered darkly, turning to leave. "I prefer to believe you merely ignorant in general."

Lord Henry stepped quickly into the breach, having just paid his respects to the dowager, who had made it patently clear she didn't know him from Adam, although she professed delight at seeing him again. "Allow me to accompany you, Miss Howland. I took your advice of the other day, you know, and procured a copy of that book at Hatchard's. Tell me, did you catch the particular irony the author demonstrated in chapter two when he described the . . ."

Lord Edward watched the pair drift away into the crowd, Lord Henry's balding head nodding up and down agitatedly as he hung on Emily Howland's every word while she answered his rapid-fire questions. *How does Monty succeed so easily with the woman, when he always fails? Perhaps he shouldn't take such joy in baiting her.* Later, Lord Edward promised Miss Howland silently; *I will see to you later.*

Turning back to his hostess, he carefully introduced himself—as always, being sure to mention that his late father was the very man who had once been brought to fight a duel for love of her more than two score years ago—and stood back to enjoy her usually incomprehensible, yet always delicious, conversation.

The dowager didn't disappoint him. "Archy's boy, of course. Dear Archy. Dead, ain't he? I could have married him, you know, but he was blond, wasn't he? I can't seem to tell blonds apart, except for dearest Georgiana, of course, as I've lived with her all of her life, and she's such a beautiful child. Girls must be easier. But the men are different somehow. They all look . . . um . . . er . . ."

"Alike?" Lord Edward supplied, wondering yet again how anyone, even Old Horry, could have forgotten his departed Papa's protuberant strawberry-red nose.

". . . alike, yes, thank you," the dowager continued happily. "It wouldn't do, would it, to be constantly forgetting what your own husband looked like. And only consider our unborn sons! Imagine how hurt they would have been if their own mama hadn't known them! Why, it might have destroyed them utterly, or at least served to *twist* them in some terrible way, if you take my meaning. You're blond, aren't you? Tell me, my dear, have you ever encountered the problem?" The dowager frowned up at him, clearly distressed for him.

"Not recently, your grace, no," he assured her, patting her hand. "Though I could consider wearing a tag with my name penned on it pinned to my jacket, I suppose."

The duchess sighed. "Oh, heavens, yes. If only everyone were so considerate. I cannot begin to tell you the trouble it would save." Then, smiling at him, she bobbed her head up and down in satisfaction. "It's good you haven't had the problem, my dear, for you seem to be such a nice boy."

Lord Edward, who was no longer a "boy," and who definitely had never before been described as being "nice," tilted his head to one side and gifted his hostess with an angelic smile. "Thank you, madam, I'm sure. Not that I don't sympathize with your difficulty concerning us blonds, of course. It must be quite taxing on your nerves."

"Oh, dear me, yes," she went on earnestly, deciding that this boy was just the sort of fellow her daughter should encourage. "You can imagine what it was like for me in the old days when everybody wore those terrible, itchy . . . um . . . er . . ."

"Wigs?"

". . . wigs, yes. A person would walk into a ballroom chock-full of nothing but flour-coated heads and black beauty patches. Of course it was impossible to *know* anyone—unless they had oddly colored eyebrows. The red ones were the most outstanding, as I remember. I think that's how I came to say yes to dearest . . . um . . . er . . . Oh, dear, how terrible! I seem to forget . . ."

"Charles, ma'am?" Lord Edward prompted

hopefully, believing the duchess to be speaking of her husband, who had been dead these fifteen years, definitely too long for her grace to have kept his name in the forefront of her mind.

"Charles? Yes, Charles—that's it! Thank you. It wasn't until I read about our engagement in the *Times* that I realized dearest Charles was a duke. I just knew that he was the lovely young man with the red eyebrows and the black star stuck to his left cheek, although I never told him, of course. He might have gotten upset."

That did it. Lord Edward choked out something about hurrying Lord Henry along with the refreshments and escaped before his sense of humor caused him to fall into public disgrace. He had planned to ingratiate himself with the duchess, who was an integral player in his plan, but it was more than obvious that buttering up Old Horry was naught but an exercise in futility. The duchess wouldn't remember him above a minute, no matter how well she thought she liked him now.

But instead of seeking out his friend, he turned his attention to ferreting out the location of Lady Georgiana among the throng of gracefully gliding dancers, easily spotting her gleaming blond head near the fringes of the polished floor, furiously fanning herself as some young fool all but drooled on her satin-clad feet.

As he had imparted to Lord Henry earlier, Lord Edward thought Lady Georgiana to be one of the most beautiful females he had ever seen, and he stopped for a moment to observe her, for he was an admirer of beautiful things. Lady Georgiana was so small, so daintily formed, so exquisitely feminine. She was, in fact, the epitome of English beauty, with soft blond curls, dimpled ivory skin, delicate roses in her cheeks, and wide emerald eyes—eyes that were quite clear and untroubled by any real intelligence.

However, with his mind and heart already otherwise engaged, all this beauty made no lasting impression on Lord Edward, though he did find it difficult to bring himself to believe Lady Georgiana was quite as cotton-headed as his friend Monty swore she was.

As he stood watching the young woman brandishing her fan to the detriment of her aspiring swain's shirt ruffles, he found himself idly thinking that it was unusual for Lord Henry to complain about this lack of brainpower, for intelligence was not usually all that high on any of Monty's or any of his friends' lists of prerequisites in choosing a mate.

After all—he knew these friends would figure—if their children had Lady Georgiana's looks and her husband's brains, those children could consider themselves well-provided-for. That it probably would not occur to the majority of these men that their offspring could conceivably have their looks and Lady Georgiana's brains—or, actually, her lack of brains—reflected only, Lord Edward believed, on their upbringing as Englishmen, and not on any real lack of common sense on their part. They were men, weren't they, and as men they had control of their own destinies. Besides, these gentlemen would doubt-less argue, Lady Georgiana was Old Horry's daughter, proving once and for all that daughters resemble their mothers, and their unborn sons would be quite safe.

He might have thought the same as his friends had his life been different, Lord Edward realized, straightening his shoulders and thanking his lucky stars that Reggie had forced him to rethink his priorities, else he might never have looked deeply enough to discover his true love. Now he had only to play out his scheme meant to return him to Lyndhurst as soon as possible, his intelligent, levelheaded, yet, he was sure, lovable prospective wife on his arm—a mission in which the adorable widgeon Lady Georgiana played a major role, whether she knew it or nay.

Smiling his most ingratiating smile, Lord Edward started forward once more, bowing and nodding his way through the throng that crowded the fringes of the dance floor, intending to whirl Lady Georgiana about the floor before he and Monty took themselves off to Lady Chilworth's game room for a space, a place less likely to contain a half-hundred marauding mamas on the hunt for fresh husband meat to toss to their man-hungry offspring.

He would then return to the ballroom later in the evening for a second dance with the beautiful young blond, preferably a waltz, just to stir up the pot a bit. After all, there was no reason to rush his fences, especially since the object of all these enterprising machinations was, regrettably, not in sight at the moment anyway.

"Lady Georgiana," he said, at last coming up behind her—and startling her so that she whirled about, narrowly missing taking a slice out of his nose with her fan as he bowed his greeting. "May I say that you are looking even more beautiful this evening than you did yesterday in the park? You must tell me your secret."

Lady Georgiana blinked her wide green eyes twice and said, a small frown appearing on her forehead, "Secret? Have you been speaking with Emily? It was only a very unexceptional bonnet, I vow, and didn't cost above forty pounds. Surely dearest Emily hasn't gone and blabbed it about to everyone?"

"Bonnet? I'm afraid I don't really understand," Lord Edward replied, tongue-in-cheek, wishing Lord Henry could hear her answer.

She playfully slapped his hand with her furled fan, making him wince as the ivory sticks made contact with his knuckles. "Oh, pooh, now you've tricked me into admitting I overspent my allowance, haven't you, Lord Edward? I thought you were remarking on the bonnet I wore yesterday on our ride. You were complimenting me, weren't you? How stupid of me not to understand."

"Now I must apologize, Lady Georgiana," Lord Edward broke in, noticing, out of the corner of his eye, that his quarry had reentered the ballroom, "as it was heartless of me to tease you. But perhaps we might take a refreshing stroll on the balcony, so that I can more fully explain my compliment." Miss Howland would be upon them at any moment to take custody of her charge, he was sure, and the relative privacy of the balcony was his choice for their next confrontation.

"Oh, that would be above all things delightful," Lady Georgiana gushed obligingly, slipping her hand through his bent arm. "It is quite warm in here, isn't it?"

The short journey to the balcony was accomplished without incident, although Lord Edward did take note of several menacing glances thrown at him by Lady Georgiana's thwarted admirers (as well as quickly spying out Miss Howland, who was in the process of rushing with controlled haste toward him and Lady Georgiana by way of the perimeter of the large ballroom, so as not to attract undue attention to the fact that her charge had somehow succeeded in slipping her leash), and they walked the length of the stone balcony before he helped her to a bench that was angled in the corner near the wall, barely into the shadows.

As he lowered his long, lean frame beside her, he said, "So, Lady Georgiana, how does it feel to be such a heartbreaker? You had them all at your feet in there, you know."

He watched as she nervously twisted her kid-encased hands together in her lap. "Oh, so you see it too!" she exclaimed, distressed. "I had hoped it wasn't so obvious. I don't know what to do. They're all so nice. Mama says they're all positively *dying* for love of me. I feel so terrible—

it's such a *responsibility*!" She turned on the seat to look up into his eyes, her own drenched with quick tears. "You don't think it will really come to that, do you? I mean, it's not as if I could possibly marry them *all*, is it?"

In another woman, these words would sound like bragging, almost like a wild American Indian who had garnered a dozen bloody scalps for his collection and was showing them off, but Lord Edward knew she was genuinely distressed by her own popularity. "I doubt you could marry above one of them, actually. I think your mother meant it merely as a figure of speech, Lady Georgiana," he said, smiling kindly.

The moment the words were out of his mouth, he knew he had erred. Drawing herself up primly, Lady Georgiana told him, "Mama doesn't speak vulgarly, sir. Figures, indeed!"

"That's not what I meant. When I said that, it was only as a figure of . . . Oh, never mind, Lady Georgiana," he said, giving it up as being beyond her. Conversation wasn't the reason he had brought her out here, and if he was right, it was just about time for Miss Howland's entrance. "Just kiss me, please, else I shall die of love for you."

Her rosebud mouth dropping open, Lady Georgiana found herself caught between worry over Lord Edward's possible demise and the knowledge that, if she were to kiss *all* the young gentlemen who spoke so—and a distressingly large number of them did—she would soon be considered "fast."

His head moving closer to hers, Lord Edward cajoled softly, "Please, dear Lady Georgiana. You know you are too kind to deny me."

Swallowing down hard on her misgivings, Lady Georgiana lifted her face to his.

3

"Just precisely what do you think you're about?"

This question, spoken in a rather loud, rather piercing tone, served to effectively halt the seated pair just as their lips were less than a whisper apart. Lord Edward remained where he was, his eyes closed tight against the sight of Lady Georgiana's companion, undoubtedly standing less than a foot in front of them, her hands stuck on her hips, a disapproving frown on her face. He was sure she was bound to be most wonderful in her righteous fury, even without looking at her. She was also, as he had predicted, exactly in the nick of time. He sent her his silent congratulations.

Lady Georgiana, however, did not possess Lord Edward's sangfroid. She quickly jerked up her head, her chin colliding with her swain's aristocratic nose with a resounding *twack* that brought a satisfied smile to Emily Howland's face, then hopped to her feet, hastily trying to wrap her Norwich shawl about her shoulders—and ended by entangling Lord Edward's handsome head (still leaning forward, still with eyes closed) in a mummy case of silken fringe.

"Oh, Emily, you startled me," Lady Georgiana said poutingly as Lord Edward fought to disengage himself from the trailing shawl, sputtering as one of the tassels found its way into his mouth.

"I'm so sorry, Georgiana," Emily said, patting her cousin's arm reassuringly. "Your mama has been asking after you, dear. Why don't you run along now and see what she wants."

"If she can remember," Lord Edward grumbled half under his breath—realizing he was not sure if he meant the duchess or her daughter—although, unfortunately, he was in the act of rising to his feet and did not notice the sparkle of amusement that flitted across Emily Howland's features before they hastily reassembled themselves in a disapproving frown.

"But, should I really leave you alone out here on the balcony with Lord Edward, Emily?" Lady Georgiana asked in some concern, seemingly oblivious of the ridiculousness of her question, considering the fact that she had just been very much isolated in this *same* spot with this *same* man. "You shouldn't be alone with him, you know, as you're unmarried and not properly chaperoned."

"Then you do at least understand the concept, Georgiana? How wonderful—how totally gratifying," Emily commented dryly, earning herself a confused look from her cousin. "But you needn't worry your pretty head about me, pet. I assure you, Lord Edward has no designs on my person."

Raising her hands to her mouth, Lady Georgiana giggled. "Oh, Emily, as if Lord Edward knew anything at all about designing ladies' gowns. You're so silly. Promise me you won't stay out here long. Bye-bye."

Emily watched until Lady Georgiana disappeared into the ballroom, then turned back to face Lord Edward, who was, in her opinion, the most foolish man in nature, considering the fact that he had chosen to remain behind on the balcony to take the sharp side of her tongue, when he could just as easily have escaped along with her cousin. "Lord Edward," Emily said by way of prologue, "I believe I have been placed in the uncomfortable role of proctor."

"Uncomfortable, Miss Howland?" Lord Edward repeated, his tone clearly implying he believed otherwise. "I would have said you look quite at home like this—on the verge of a scathing lecture."

"How amusing, my lord," Emily drawled, clearly more than halfway convinced that someone, somehow, should do this abominable creature an injury for his audaciousness. "Surely you realize that what you have done is totally reprehensible?"

"I don't know how that could be, Miss Howland, as you interrupted me before I could *do* anything," he informed her matter-of-factly, running a hand through his hair to be sure the passage of the shawl over it hadn't reworked its style from casual to careless. "Besides, it was totally innocent, and only in the nature of an experiment."

"Indeed." The single word held within it a world of meaning—and contempt. "How utterly heartless of me to interrupt, and just as you were about to make a breakthrough in your research, I'm sure. Can you ever find it in your heart to forgive me?"

"There's no need for sarcasm, Miss Howland," Lord Edward told her, straightening his jacket. "Kindly just proceed in tearing a strip off my hide and have done with it, please. I have to hurry away if I hope to debauch my usual three innocents before dawn."

"Please, my lord, bragging is so tedious. Are your intentions concerning my cousin honorable?"

The question, uttered so calmly, took him by surprise. He stopped the inventory of his attire to look at her, half-expecting to see that he was now being held at pistol point, but she was standing there quite calmly, awaiting his answer. Pluck to the backbone, that was his Miss Howland, and Lord Edward's opinion of her mettle went up another notch.

Emily was a tall woman—an important factor, considering his own above-average height— yet she always seemed somehow to accomplish a way of looking shorter, almost dumpy. Her heavy reddish-brown hair was done in the same mass of intricate, upswept curls as her cousin's, with none of the blond's resultant charm. Her skin appeared sallow, almost yellow, against the gray of her high-necked gown, and her strangely slanted brown eyes and winglike brows followed the same line as her high, prominent cheekbones, giving her face an exotic, almost foreign look. No, it wouldn't have surprised him if she had been holding a pistol.

Yet, with his discerning eye, Lord Edward knew that Emily Howland was basically a fine-looking woman, and had known it from his first sight of her a month earlier. Her hair was all wrong, of course, while her clothing was nothing short of atrocious, and her choice of colors ... well, that he considered to be downright criminal. But this was all secondary and easily mended.

The dumpiness concerned him slightly more, although he was sure she probably only overate to compensate for her miserable position in life. After all, being a poor relation was no picnic in the park, and bear-leading the childlike Lady Georgiana while trying to make heads or tails of the dowager duchess had to take its toll somewhere. No, Lord Edward wasn't overly concerned with Emily's present looks. Not when she possessed such a fine mind, such a level head, and, most important, such a boundless affection and patience for her brainless relatives.

Perhaps if he were to tell her the truth, come smack out into the open with his real intentions, she would ... But no, not yet. She wouldn't believe he really loved her, for one thing, and she might believe he only wanted to use her, for another. He'd have to bide his time until he could somehow manage to get the dowager to come to Lyndhurst Hall for a house party at the conclusion of the Season. After all, much as he was sure Emily was the one he wanted, there was still Reggie to consider. He had to see Emily and Reggie together, and then . . . well, everything would just quite naturally fall into place, without his ever having to tell her that he—

"My goodness, my lord, have you somehow mislaid your agile tongue?" Emily asked, interrupting his rambling thoughts. "I should think my question direct enough. What *are* your intentions?"

"Excuse me, Miss Howland, if your rudeness took me aback for a moment. My intentions, ma'am, as you were so impolite as to ask, are to quit this balcony and this ridiculous conversation as soon as may be. Now, if you don't mind—"

"But I *do* mind, Lord Edward," Emily said, stepping in front of him to block his path. "I don't like you, sir, as I'm sure you already know. I don't like you one bit, and my opinion of you is even lower now that I realize you are fully aware of the extreme innocence of my cousin Georgiana. She is naught but a babe, no matter if she is nearly eighteen. Do you think I didn't hear that drivel you were pouring into her ears? Dying for love, indeed. As if you could possibly love such an infant! She is years away from marriage. Please, credit me with at least that much intelligence. If you *were* to marry her, you'd strangle her within the week."

"I imagine this lecture has a point," Lord Edward drawled, adjusting his shirt cuff so that he had something else to think of than his sudden overwhelming need to kiss her.

"The point, Lord Edward, as you so crudely put it, is that I want you to stay away from my cousin. I just left my aunt, and she was waxing poetic about that 'handsome blond boy somebody-or-other' who would be perfect for her Georgy. They're numbskulls, the two of them, but they're *my* numbskulls, and I won't have you hurting them."

"You're so loyal, Miss Howland," Lord Edward said, complimenting her, advancing so that she involuntarily stepped back a pace. Prudence be damned! The woman was driving him insane. If only she weren't acting as Lady Georgiana's chaperone. How could a person properly court a female who wouldn't dance, or drive out with him, or even go down to dinner with him so that they could get to know each other? It was about time he made her aware of him as a man who was capable of looking at her in a romantic light. "Perhaps I am pursuing the wrong female entirely," he continued, taking another step toward her, aware of a light buzzing in his ears. "Do you mind if I conduct another small experiment?"

"What . . . what do you think you're doing?" Emily squeaked, suddenly not so sure of herself, and she looked about hastily for some means of escape. It was no good. She had somehow succeeded in backing herself into a corner.

Lord Edward's hands grabbed Emily at the shoulders and he hauled her up against his chest as his mouth swooped down to cover hers. He ground his lips against hers passionately, his wide-open green eyes staring unblinkingly into her wide-open brown ones, in order to gauge her reaction. He slanted his mouth first one way, then the other, without ever breaking contact, employing all of his considerable romantic skill, feeling his teeth scrape lightly against hers, his hands leaving her shoulders to crush her against him from knee to breast.

It was no use. She didn't react, didn't fight him, didn't swoon. She just stood there, locked within the circle of his arms, and *glared* at him. He released her with a rush of pent-up breath, turning away in mingled chagrin and self-disgust. "I'm sorry," he muttered angrily, and he was— sorry for having succumbed to impulse, and angry for having failed so miserably in his attempt to bend her to his will.

Emily stood ramrod straight, still trapped in her corner, magnificently dowdy in her ugly gray gown, and stared out over the darkened gardens. "You may leave me now, please," she said, her voice sounding strained but unwavering.

Lord Edward reached out a hand to touch her arm, then dropped it. "I don't know what came over me just now, Miss Howland, I really don't. I've never forced myself on anyone before. It's just . . . it's just . . . well, you see, I just wanted to . . ."

"Is your hearing as well as your judgment impaired, then, Lord Edward? I have asked that you leave me." Emily's hands were drawn into tight fists at her sides as she struggled to maintain her composure. She was twenty, no schoolroom miss, but if he didn't take himself off so that she could collapse on the bench and give way to the storm of weeping that was building up behind her eyes, she would never forgive him.

"If you'd just allow me to apologize—"

"Apology heard and accepted, Lord Edward," she cut in shortly. "Now, please, go!"

"I'll stay away from Lady Georgiana as well, I promise," he offered weakly, not knowing what else to say. "You're right, you know, she is just an infant. You're prudent to guard her so closely."

Emily only nodded, unable to trust her voice.

"I am really seriously thinking of marrying, you know. I need to set up my nursery."

"Oh, really? Then I can see your reasoning in pursuing my cousin. With Georgy already installed in your town house, it would simply be a matter of tossing in a rocking horse and a set of blocks to make this nursery of yours complete. Georgy would have been deliriously happy, although you might have found that you were still lacking a wife." Emily was being sarcastic again—and at her cousin's expense, too—but she couldn't help herself. She simply couldn't believe Lord Edward would possibly consider Lady Georgiana in the role of his wife. It was ludicrous. Perhaps she *had* underestimated his intelligence.

"The knife is already firmly in, Miss Howland. There's no need to twist the blade," Lord Edward said, turning to walk away. "Actually," he added, believing he might as well be hanged for a sheep as a lamb, "I believe I must rethink my requirements for a wife. I'm definitely more intrigued with feminine wit than I had supposed I would be. Now it is up to me to find a young woman with dear Lady Georgiana's gentle heart and your keen intellect, and my search will be over."

And with that final insult, Lord Edward removed himself from the balcony, to search out Lord Henry and retire to a private gaming club where, knowing his plans had just suffered a major setback—and out of his own mouth, no less—he proceeded to get himself well and truly drunk.

4

⚓

The Chilworth drawing room was overrun with flowers, towering formal arrangements filling the air with their perfume while overloading the side tables and overshadowing the smaller, more informal clutches of posies sent by Lady Georgiana's less-plump-in-the-pocket swains, who hoped their offerings would be considered to be "romantic" rather than merely purse-pinched.

It was the same in the foyer, the morning room, the small salon, and the music room. Everywhere Emily Howland went the morning after the ball, she was confronted with overblown roses, dainty daffodils, exotic orchids, and blushing violets. In an effort to escape the riot of color and cloying scent, she slipped into Lady Georgiana's ermine-hooded cloak that she found lying forgotten in the morning room, pulled open the double glass doors that led onto the balcony, and skipped lightly down the flagstones into the garden.

"At least there are less flowers out here than

inside," she commented aloud facetiously before seating herself in her private hideaway on a curved stone bench that had been placed just in front of the length of hedge that separated the garden from the tradesmen's entrance. It was early, and the dew still clung to the grass, dampening her shoes, so that she slipped out of them and tucked her feet up under her skirts, knowing she was being unladylike, but not believing anyone cared overmuch what poor relations did anyway.

The sun went behind a cloud and it began to drizzle, which was not unusual for London in the spring—or London at any time of year, she thought, for, indeed, she was not in the most charitable of moods—but still she lingered on the bench, glorying in the peace and quiet she had been seeking. It was nearly noon, and although Emily had been up and about for several hours, having spent a short, uncomfortable night filled with unpleasant dreams, her aunt and cousin had not yet stirred beyond allowing themselves to be propped up in bed with cups of chocolate and the morning post.

At least two dozen eager gentlemen callers come to continue their impassioned wooing of Lady Georgiana had already been turned away unseen, Emily's insincere apologies obviously not soothing them in the least, and she absolutely refused to feel guilty over deserting her post and allowing the Chilworth butler to bear the brunt of any other callers' disappointment in her stead.

Yes, it would take more than some damp and drizzle to oust Emily from her hiding place.

She needed time alone, time to think, although why her thought processes should be clearer this morning than they had been during the night, she had no idea. Drat that insufferable Lord Edward anyhow! How dare he insult her the way he had? She knew she was no beauty, but she certainly didn't need his snide remarks to put a final seal of certainty on the matter. And that kiss! Why, he couldn't have been any meaner, any more insulting, if he had slapped her face.

Emily decided all over again that she didn't like Lord Edward Laurence. She didn't like him at all.

On the half-dozen or so occasions she had been forced into the man's company—acting as an uncomfortable third whenever he came to see Lady Georgiana—she had concluded that he was reckless, feckless, and totally lacking in responsibility. He treated life as if it were one huge frolic, which she acknowledged must be easy enough to do, what with no wars left to be fought, a comfortable title, and endless wealth cushioning him from the realities of everyday life, while the entire city of London was his own personal sporting ground.

Besides, he was simply too perfect, too handsome for his own good—or for hers.

For one thing, he had the most beautiful green eyes she had ever seen. Not deeply emerald, like Georgy's, but a light, tender, new-leaf green, with flecks of morning sunlight forever dancing in them—a sparkle put there, she was sure, only to infuriate her, as she wondered just what was going on inside his head.

She moved uncomfortably on the stone seat, not liking where her thoughts were taking her, but unable to stop their travels.

His hair was darkly blond, almost the exact shade of the honey her mother harvested from the bees at her home in Surrey, rather than the bright guinea yellow of Georgy's, and more than once Emily had had to fight down the impulse to brush back the one errant lock that continually slipped down onto his forehead.

And those beautiful, even white teeth; ah, he had a glorious, mischievous smile. His body was perfect, not at all dissipated, as he was a renowned, if somewhat undisciplined sportsman, and his mode of dress was fashionable without being silly.

Her hands, carefully folded in her lap, clenched into tight fists.

He had everything.

She had nothing.

To be without, to be forever on the outside looking in, was one thing; to have the insufferable Lord Edward going to such lengths to bring her shortcomings to her attention—as he had done with such devastating effect last night—was unspeakable.

Lord, how she loathed him.

And now he was actually setting himself at her silly, lovable cousin Georgy.

Oh, he may have tried to fob her off—tried to worm his way out of his scandalous behavior toward a young woman of quality by saying he had erred in believing her cousin would make him a good wife—but Emily found it hard to swallow that particular story.

After all, they *did* make a beautiful couple, almost dazzling in their combined beauty, and when it came to a female as beautiful as Lady Georgiana, her one shortcoming—a total lack of brainpower—was simple to overlook. Even if her cousin weren't the most perfect collection of skin, bone, and hair to appear in London in three decades, her wealth and title were ample inducement for any suitor.

If only Lady Georgiana weren't the youngest of five daughters. Then her grace would hold out for someone of higher rank than Lord Edward Laurence, a younger son, to take her baby off her hands. But the dowager was growing weary of the social round, and eager to settle Georgy and get back to her comfortable country estate, where she already knew everyone's name (except those of her many grandchildren, but the dowager didn't believe anyone under the age of fifty counted for much in the scheme of things anyway).

Hadn't her aunt said only last night that she believed Lord Edward to be a vastly suitable catch? Emily shook her head and sighed. She was only deluding herself if she believed her grace would ever see through the man as she did. It was all but settled; dear birdwitted Georgy and the insufferable Lord Edward would probably be affianced before the week was out.

"Unless . . . unless someone can somehow discover a way to get through to Aunt Hortense and convince her that Georgy and Lord Edward definitely would not suit."

The moment Emily voiced the thought aloud, she realized that she was that "someone." It made perfect sense. She was close to both Lady Georgiana and the dowager duchess; she was a trusted family member; she had—thanks to her dear optimistic mother, who thought serving as companion to Georgy would land Emily a husband of her own—made herself invaluable to both the Chilworth ladies ever since they had moved to Portman Square for the Season.

She was the obvious, the only choice. But how was she to discredit Lord Edward to her aunt and cousin? Whatever Lord Edward was, whatever he did, he was accepted by the *ton*, even idolized by it.

It wouldn't be enough to drop a few veiled hints in her aunt's ear about the man's title of Naughty Ned, for such things were looked on most kindly by the older generation, who could only relive their more rakish juvenile exploits vicariously through such nonsense. And as much as Emily wished it were possible, she couldn't say that the man was actually dishonest in any way, or some such thing.

No, she'd have to think of something else, something so terrible, so completely damning, that Aunt Hortense, aghast, would have him banned from the house forevermore, an action that would go a long way to making Emily's life easier, for his presence seemed to fill her head with the oddest, almost embarrassing pictures. Emily sat and sat, as the drizzle turned the borrowed cloak sodden and heavy with moisture. She thought and thought, her slanted brown eyes narrowed into thin slits as she concentrated on her scheme.

At last, just as a cold drop of water slid off the fur to land on the tip of her nose, a small smile came onto Emily's face, and she tilted her head slightly to one side, considering the germ of an idea.

An absolutely wonderful ... awful ... sneaky ... *glorious* idea.

"Yes-s-s," she hissed from between clenched teeth. "It could work; it just could work. What does it matter what happens to my reputation? After all, I am only a poor relation, an unpaid companion. Once Georgy is safely settled, I'll be packed back off to Surrey, where I will then apply myself to being a comforting prop to my widowed mother in her declining years—to nurse my as-yet-unborn nephews and nieces through the croup, and sundry other such wild exploits indulged in by aging, on-the-shelf spinsters. It could even lend some cachet to my supposed tormented past for me to giggle over as I tend my cats. I'm sure I'll have cats," she added for no particular reason other than the fact that she liked to be clear about things, "as they're much less trouble than temperamental lapdogs."

Her decision made, Emily rose to return to the house. "Besides," she added, just to convince herself of the rightness of her plan, "it's not as if the story would go any further than Aunt Hortense's boudoir. Yes, if it comes to that, if I find I am left with no other choice, I'll do it. Anything—anything!—to thwart that nefarious Ned!"

5

Meanwhile, the gentleman Emily Howland considered to be the villain of the piece, one Lord Edward Mortimer Sinclair Laurence, was propped inelegantly in a dreadfully uncomfortable wooden armchair in the small dining room of his town house in Half Moon Street, nursing his tender head with a strong cup of coffee and wondering just what it was that he had done the previous evening that had made it mandatory he have visited upon him this morning all the terrible demons too much drink could conjure up to persecute a person.

His tongue silently complained that his mouth was a quite inhospitable residence, as it seemed to have shrunk overnight and could no longer adequately house its lifelong resident, while his tongue itself was far from a matter of joy to him, being curiously fur-covered and desert dry.

His brainbox, that part of him that seemed to rise three feet above his eyebrows (and twice as wide), had been somehow rendered a near-blank,

47

telling him only that he hurt abominably and that he must have been a bad boy—a very, very bad boy indeed.

He sipped at his coffee, nearly bending in half over the tabletop so that his weary arms shouldn't have to heft the cup, promising himself that if he lived—and at the moment, he felt this possibility to be in some serious doubt—he would never, never, *never* touch another drop of whatever it was he had poured down his throat the night before.

"If only I could remember what it was," he murmured quietly, wincing as his words echoed inside his ears like hammer blows on an anvil.

With his eyes squeezed tightly closed—the darkness behind his lids serving as a canvas upon which his headache painted a colorful fireworks display to put Prinny's elaborate peace celebrations to the blush—his mind's eye slowly conjured up the horrific vision of two widely open, curiously slanted brown eyes.

These eyes, obviously condemning, definitely scornful, looked deep inside him, straight through to his guilty soul. And although they were eyes, and certainly not to be thought able to speak, these particular eyes began a curious chant, taunting over and over: "Coward, coward, coward."

"Oh, Lord," he groaned, finally remembering. "Emily. Good grief, what have I done?"

"Shot the cat about a half-dozen times, at least according to your man, Burton. I passed him in the hall, lugging a suspicious-looking bucket and wearing his usual disapproving frown. You and Monty really must have made a night of it, Ned. You haven't been the worse for liquor in years. Is she someone I know?"

Lord Edward lifted his throbbing eyelids a fraction to look across the table to where Lord Delbert Updegrove was in the process of lowering his tall Norse-warrior frame into the facing chair and said urbanely, "Go to the devil, Del, old sport, would you?"

"Oh-ho! Struck a nerve, did I? Monty said something about you being all arsy-varsy over The Chilworth, but I didn't believe him. I mean, Georgy's turned out to be rather beautiful—quite angelic, actually—but there's definitely no problem of overcrowding in her upper rooms, is there? Grew up smack next door to her in Sussex, you know, and I can't say as how she ever impressed me to the point I'd get myself cupshot over her. All the Chilworth females take after the mother, and we all know what a peagoose Old Horry is. Lord, the stories I could tell you!"

"Maybe I was thinking of fixing my interest with her," Lord Edward hinted to his friend, finally finding the courage to sit back in his chair. "Did you ever think of that?" Del looked disgustingly fit, from his fiery red thatch of hair to his crisp canary-yellow waistcoat and sky-blue jacket—which was as much of him that Lord Edward could or, at the moment, cared to see. He frowned, convinced his old friend looked like a mis-hued robin redbreast.

"Marry Old Horry?" Lord Delbert shook his

head in disbelief. "That's where the money is, of course. But you do realize people are bound to talk."

"No, you dolt, not the dowager. Lady Georgiana." Yes, Lord Edward decided, I'm being punished. Anyone would think Miss Howland sent Del over here purposely to pummel me with his inane nonsense.

Lord Delbert poured out some steaming coffee for himself and then reached for the cream pot, promptly spilling it. "Whoops! Dashed clumsy of me, what? Well, glad to hear it, Ned. Makes sense, seeing as how you'd want an heir. You'll get no foals from the old gal. She's past it, you know. Ah, thank you, Burton."

Burton, who had brought the extra cup into the dining room, and who was standing by, his nose appearing just above the tabletop, waiting for the accident to happen (with Lord Delbert it was not a question of whether or not there would be a mishap, but only of when it would occur), flourished a linen serviette he took from his apron pocket and promptly set about cleaning up the spill. "No trouble at all, m'lord," he assured him, deftly removing the marmalade— the preserves being so apt to stain—from his lordship's reach and personally spooning some onto a muffin for him.

Watching this little interchange, Lord Edward concluded that it wasn't necessary to clear up Lord Delbert's misconception about exactly which of the Chilworth women he had supposedly planned to wed. It came to him next to discuss the dreaded "Incident on the Balcony" with his friend, and it only served to highlight the extreme distress in which Lord Edward found himself this morning that he even considered entering into such a delicate matter with the affable but vague redhead.

"I kissed Miss Howland last night," Naughty Ned said baldly, his treacherous tongue acting with more alacrity than his sore brain.

Bits of marmalade and muffin shot into the air, lingering there for a second—like thistles caught in the spring breeze—then settled on the fine linen tablecloth, dotting its surface with colorful starlike stains as Lord Delbert, his eyes popped wide with incredulity, coughed and choked, trying to regain his breath.

Burton cursed, but only softly, as he *was*, after all, a gentleman's gentleman as well as a butler, and quickly went to work cleaning up the mess.

Not so Lord Delbert. *"You what!"* His face an unbecoming puce—and clashing badly with his hair—Lord Delbert leaned forward, bug-eyed, looking at his friend as if the fellow had somehow sprouted antlers. *"Are you out of your mind?"*

Lord Edward, knowing himself to be guilty as sin, took refuge in pettishness. "It wasn't all my fault, Del. She goaded me into it," he complained, thrusting out his bottom lip so that Burton, who had been with the Laurence family three dozen years or more, rolled his eyes and felt himself hard-pressed not to cuff the young master's ears. In the end, he settled for lifting the heavy silver teapot and then slamming it down heavily on the tabletop, three inches from his lordship's elbow, thereby warning his master not to give the whole game away.

Clapping both his hands to the sides of his head, Lord Edward let out a long, low, slowly spoken string of nastiness that did nothing to enlighten the usually indiscreet Lord Delbert as to his friend's hidden motives concerning one Miss Emily Howland, but did serve to satisfy something deep in his own soul.

When it was done, and after Burton, sniffing his disgust, had quit the room, slamming the door behind him as he went, Lord Delbert rewarded his friend by applauding softly, saying, "An inspired monologue, Ned. I really should have asked Burton to take notes, as I always seem to run out of curses beforetimes. I take it Georgy's resident she-dragon tackled you in the hedges?"

"She's not a she-dragon, Del," Lord Edward was stung into retorting. "As a matter of fact, she appeals to me most extremely. And you have it the wrong way round; I attacked *her*—out on the balcony." Then, knowing he had just made another major error in judgment, but also knowing it was too late to do anything about it, he stuffed half a muffin in his mouth and glared at his friend.

Lord Delbert sat back in his chair and inspected his friend's expression. "You really mean that, don't you, Ned? You really are attracted to Miss Howland. I can't see it, to tell you the truth, but if you say it's so, I guess it isn't up to me to question it, is it? Only one thing, Ned. If you're after the she-dra ... I mean, Miss Howland, aren't you going about the thing all backwards? I mean, Monty told me you were after Georgy."

"Miss Howland doesn't like me," Lord Edward replied, as if that explained everything, which it didn't, as Lord Delbert's confused frown clearly showed. "I'm using Lady Georgiana to stay in Miss Howland's company," was all Lord Edward added, thinking his plot too deep for his friend to understand.

A few weeks later, thinking back over this particular conversation, Lord Edward was to reassess his friend's capacity for deep thinking—if only to attempt to discover exactly how the affable redhead had come to leap to such a ridiculous conclusion.

6

Lady Imogene Carstairs had prudently limited the invitations to her Venetian breakfast to include no more than three hundred and fifty of the most important of the *ton*, which of course meant that nearly twice that number of people—those others being servants, chefs, coachmen, ladies' companions, and sundry other persons of no social consequence but completely necessary to the success of the day—descended pell-mell on Richmond Park just before noon, intent on enjoying themselves with a bit of frolic in the fine spring sunshine.

Lady Georgiana particularly enjoyed informal outings of this sort, feeling so much closer in spirit to her beloved home in Sussex when out and about in the open spaces, where she could breathe clean, crisp country air and, when no one was looking, slide her feet out of her tight silk slippers and wiggle her bare toes in the cool grass.

London was wonderful—a fairyland, really—

just as her dearest mama had promised, and she would have been a silly thing indeed not to adore all the attention she was receiving, but Lady Georgiana was at heart a simple country miss, more at home in familiar surroundings, where she was not forever being poked at by pushy seamstresses or being ogled by silly gentlemen who insisted upon treating her as if she were a particularly fragile crystal vase, and liable to shatter at the slightest jostle.

Emily, on the other hand, who firmly believed she had seen enough bucolic countryside in her twenty years to last her three lifetimes, was bored to flinders. Not that she didn't like the country, for she did, but town life was so much more interesting and exciting.

A person could find no end of things to do in London, what with the theater and the museums and the lending libraries and the centuries of history that confronted her at every turn. She imagined she would even like the social round, if she were to be in Lady Georgiana's position and able to enjoy all the excitement firsthand, rather than merely being allowed to observe it from a chair pushed against the wall, where she never failed to find herself jammed in between two flabby-armed, perspiring, foul-breathed dowagers.

Not that she was on the hunt for a husband. Good heavens, no! Emily was much too levelheaded to even consider such a wild, improbable possibility. She was nothing like her optimistic mother, who had confided her dream that her oldest child was going to take the town by storm. *She* was a realist. She had absolutely no fortune, and certainly didn't believe herself to have been blessed with any great beauty. She knew that, as far as the marriage stakes were concerned, she was what was considered to be a dark horse.

An also-ran.

"A nag," she added aloud ruefully, reluctantly rising from her comfortable seat beneath a leafy tree to go chasing after her unwitting cousin, who was carelessly allowing Lord Hetherson entirely too much license as they strolled together near a small stream. It was one thing to allow the man to grasp her elbow as they walked along the uneven bank, Emily decided, but it was quite another matter entirely for Lady Georgiana to laugh up into his eyes as the fellow pretended to stumble while covertly slipping an arm around her waist.

After deftly removing her cousin from Lord Hetherson's clutches, *tsk-tsking* at the blushing young man over her shoulder as she walked away, Emily quickly guided Lady Georgiana back to the shade tree, lecturing her halfheartedly and feeling as if she were back home in Surrey, riding herd on one of her young siblings. Being the eldest child was not easy, but at least it had prepared her for her current position, and she quickly employed an oft-used practice—diverting the childlike Lady Georgiana from possible mischief by offering her a treat.

"You really will, Emily? Oh, that would be

the best of good fun," Lady Georgiana trilled, skipping alongside her cousin, having completely forgotten poor Lord Hetherson. "I do so love daisy chains, but I have never been able to make one that looks like anything. I never seem to leave the stems long enough, and by the time I'm done my fingers are all green and the lovely flowers are all sad and drooping and I feel awful—as if I'm a *murderer* or something."

Seating herself once more on the carriage blanket that had been spread out for them by one of the army of servants that was now busily setting up more substantial seating in the middle of a large open area nearby, Emily picked up one of the flowers she had gathered earlier in order to occupy herself, then waited patiently as Lady Georgiana's attention was diverted yet again by a passing juggler Lady Imogene had thoughtfully provided to amuse her guests.

"It's really quite easy to lace the flowers together, Georgy. Let me teach you. Georgy, please, you're no longer a child!" Emily scolded at last, as her cousin appeared about to scamper off after the performer, who, Emily noticed, had winked at the lovely young blond.

"Oh, pooh, Cousin," Lady Georgiana pouted prettily, giving the departing juggler one last wistful look. "You're no fun, Emmy. You're no fun at all. We were just having the nicest little talk."

Emily sighed, patting the place next to her. "Yes, I'm sure you were. Sit down now, dear, and we'll make your chain together, and then

you can make one for me. Won't that be fun?"
Honestly, she thought, keeping her smile firmly
in place, I do believe it would be easier all
round if I could just put the dratted child on
leading strings.

The two young women busied themselves for
a few minutes on slitting the stems of the flowers just so and then stringing them together,
Emily's capable hands working deftly, while Lady
Georgiana looked endearingly befuddled as she
struggled with her recalcitrant blooms, her small
pink tongue protruding from the corner of her
mouth as she concentrated all her effort on the
task.

It seemed a perfect time for Emily to sound
out her cousin's emotions about a particular
person of their acquaintance. "How do you *really*
feel about Lord Edward Laurence, Georgy?" she
asked after a while, keeping her voice deliberately casual. "I realized too late that I might
have been interrupting him the other evening
just as he was about to favor you with a proposal."

"No, you're wrong, Emmy," Lady Georgiana
replied, going nearly cross-eyed as she raised
two flowers to her face in order to thread one
through the other. "He had already made his
proposal before you came along." She giggled
innocently, believing she was about to make a
dashing good joke. "He had *proposed* to kiss
me—and he would have, too, if you hadn't come
along and discovered us."

Emily pinched the bridge of her nose between
her thumb and index finger, feeling a headache

coming on. Lady Georgiana might not be too bright, but she was definitely all female. "And did you *want* Lord Edward to kiss you, Georgy?" she prompted, fearing her cousin's answer.

Lady Georgiana shrugged, and one of the flowers fell to her lap, minus its stem. "Oh, drat! I told you I couldn't do this. Mama says I have six thumbs. Did you see those slippers I embroidered for her, Emmy? They're just *awful.*"

"Georgy, just answer the question, please." Emily still hadn't put her plan into motion, most probably, she told herself, because she dreaded the interview with her aunt, who was bound to take forever to realize even half of what her niece was saying, confusing the issue until Emily would be forced to draw the dear dense lady a diagram; but if she found that Georgy wasn't seriously interested in Lord Edward, the entire project might be abandoned and she could save herself any amount of trouble.

"Did I want him to kiss me?" Lady Georgiana repeated, a small frown marring her smooth forehead. "I really don't know exactly, Emily. He *said* he was dying with love for me, which, you have to admit, was extremely nice of him. But then they *all* say they're in love with me, and I can't go about kissing them all, can I? I think I felt sorry for him, to tell you the truth. He was being so sweet. Yes, I felt sorry for him. There—look, Emmy, I finally got two of them to stay together!"

Oh, that's just above all things marvelous, Emily thought, despairing, even as she applauded her cousin's small success. Her cousin felt sorry for Lord Edward. For someone like Lady Georgiana, it would be a short hop from feeling sorry for a man to marrying him, just to make the poor fellow happy. She had a good, caring heart, Lady Georgiana did, but she wasn't very logical. "Do you realize, Georgy, that Lord Edward nearly compromised you out there on the balcony? I mean, your mother has explained such things to you, hasn't she?"

"Of course she has, you silly thing," Lady Georgiana averred, blushing hotly as she poked her cousin in the ribs. "That's one of the reasons I don't let *any* of them kiss me above once. I'm not so careless as my sister Henrietta, you know. Henrietta was compromised, you understand, although it's a great big secret," she whispered conspiratorially. "That's how she came to marry that awful Peregrine. Mama told me all about it—the way Perry kissed her and all. The baby's very sweet, though, so it isn't all that bad, is it?"

Obviously Lady Georgiana's education in the ways of procreation was woefully incomplete, but Emily didn't feel it to be her place to enlighten her. As a matter of fact, she thought hopefully, she might just be able to use this particular "misconception" for her own ends. "And would you want to have Lord Edward's child, Georgy?" she asked, watching her cousin's face closely, and receiving exactly the opposite reaction from the one she had hoped to engender.

"A child? I . . . I never actually thought about it. A child," she repeated slowly, her features going all soft and dreamy—just as Emily's features showed signs of pinching, realizing that she had made another gross tactical error. Of course Georgy would want a child—all children enjoy playing with dolls! And as if to prove the point, Lady Georgiana gushed, "Wouldn't that be sweet of Lord Edward? I just adore children, Emily. I could teach her how to sit a pony, and we could go into the village together so she could play with all the other children beside the pond, the way I used to do." She turned to Emily, her vivid green eyes dancing with childish delight. "Is that what you mean?"

Good Lord, no, that's precisely what I *don't* mean, Emily thought wretchedly, but if we were to sit here until the first frost, I would never be able to explain so you would understand. Knowing she was being a coward, Emily explained, fingers crossed, "You would have to live with Lord Edward, sweetheart. You do realize that, don't you? You'd have to leave Chilworth Manor forever and ever if you were to become his wife."

Lady Georgiana's full lower lip pushed out as she digested this sad fact. "I don't ever want to leave my home—not ever! How horrid of Lord Edward to even suggest it. And I thought he liked me! Well, let me tell you, I shan't speak to that man again! Imagine that—to leave my beloved Chilworth Manor! That's horrible! Thank you so much for explaining it all to me. I told Mama I didn't think I wanted a London Season, but she insisted, you know, saying that she longed for some peace in her dotage, or something like that. Isn't it strange that she didn't tell me I'd have to leave Chilworth Manor? After all, Henrietta didn't. I shall *never* marry now."

Emily placed the completed daisy chain atop her cousin's blond curls, then gave Lady Georgiana a heartfelt kiss on the cheek. "I doubt that, my sweet, but I must admit I really am glad to hear that you aren't considering Lord Edward as a possible mate. You two really wouldn't suit, you know."

"Oh, dear. We wouldn't?"

"As a matter of fact," Emily concluded, just to add the finishing icing to the top of the cake of fibs and half-truths she had single-handedly constructed, "I understand that Lord Edward dislikes children—and that he absolutely *loathes* the country, preferring to spend all of his time in town." Carousing and making a terrible nuisance of himself, she added to herself silently.

"Oh, dear," Lady Georgiana repeated (for her vocabulary was not extensive), stiffening and grabbing on to her cousin's forearm. "There he is now, and I believe he's coming this way." To think, he was almost the father of her child! She was embarrassed beyond reason. "Oh, Emily, I don't think I can face him, really I don't. Please, do something!"

Emily carefully disengaged herself from her cousin's fierce grip, looking out over the area to see Lord Edward advancing purposefully across the grass—just as she had thought he would, just as if he had never promised to stop chasing after Lady Georgiana—Lord Delbert Updegrove and Lord Henry Montgomery flanking him on either side. Younger sons, the three of them, devoid of responsibility but all with fine old names and solid incomes to cushion them, they moved with a self-confidence that had Emily clenching her jaws until her teeth ached.

"Good afternoon, ladies," Lord Edward said in greeting, stopping just in front of the blanket and doffing his curly-brimmed beaver to bow with a courtly flourish, his companions quickly following suit. "May I say, Lady Georgiana, that you make a veritable picture sitting here, putting Dame Nature to shame with your beauty."

Well, that puts *me* firmly in my place, doesn't it? Emily thought, feeling herself beginning to wilt even as she wondered why she was upset that he was ignoring her when she should be doing celebratory handsprings that he was.

Lady Georgiana giggled, modestly holding her hand to her mouth as she rolled her eyes at the gentlemen. "Aren't you sweet! Aren't they sweet, Emmy? They're so sweet. Please, sit down."

Emily too rolled her eyes, but for quite another reason. So much for Georgy's fear of Lord Edward, she thought resignedly, carefully gathering her skirts about her to make room for Lord Delbert, whose wide, athletic frame took up a good third of the blanket.

"Georgy, you're looking fine as ninepence these days," Lord Delbert told her with the ease of long acquaintance. "I hardly know you without a smudge on your cheek from climbing trees. Lord, Monty, you wouldn't believe what a ragtag urchin Georgy used to be, following us boys around back home, nipping at our heels like a puppydog. But you've grown up real fine, honest, Georgy."

This faint praise served to happily remind Lady Georgiana that Lord Delbert—whom she had always considered to be the older brother she never had—lived almost on top of her mother's comfortable dower house on the edge of the Chilworth estate. Wasn't she a silly goose! Why hadn't she thought of Delbert before? Leaning across Emily so that she could peer intently into his lordship's rather vacant blue eyes, she questioned pointedly: "Do *you* like children, Del?"

Emily's chin dropped onto her chest in defeat, a reaction that did not go unnoticed by Lord Edward, who had covertly been watching her out of the corners of his eyes ever since he sat down. Something was going on here, of that he was sure, but he hadn't the slightest notion what it was. This lack of knowledge, of course, did not stop him from putting his own oar in before Lord Delbert, who was looking momentarily stunned, could form an answer to Lady Georgiana's question.

"Yes, Del, tell us, do," Lord Edward prodded playfully from his comfortable position, stretched out full length on his side upon the ground, his head supported by one hand as he absently twirled a daisy beneath his aristocratic nose. "You cannot imagine the sleepless nights I have spent wondering the same about you myself."

Lord Delbert, coloring to the roots of his red hair, shifted himself in embarrassment, unconsciously leaning his hand painfully against Emily's foot as he rearranged his bulk, causing her to inhale sharply and wonder if everyone from Sussex was clumsy or if she might have at last stumbled on the perfect mate for her accident-prone cousin. "Of course I like children," he protested hotly. "Doesn't everyone? What a silly question, Georgy. And here I thought you were all grown-up."

Seeing that Lady Georgiana was about to defend her question—and doubtless reveal her earlier conversation with her cousin in order to explain her reasoning—Emily stepped quickly into the breach by turning to ask Lord Henry, "Was that a new pair I saw you up behind yesterday in the park, Lord Henry? They were quite beautiful."

Lord Henry, who was known to have less knowledge about horseflesh than anyone in the world did of the composition of the moon, found himself to be inordinately pleased that Miss Howland had commented favorably on his latest purchase. "I picked them up at Tatt's just this past week, ma'am," he told her importantly as Lord Delbert snorted his poor opinion of the flashy grays. "Chose them myself, personally."

"Which explains why they can't move above a trot without jostling you out of your seat," Lord Edward slid in, still looking at Emily. Something havey-cavey was going on—her cowhanded attempt at diversion proved it—and he quickly brought the conversation back to the point. "Do *you* like children, Lady Georgiana?"

"Yes, I do," she told him, her lovely eyes narrowed as she looked at him in patent dislike. "I absolutely adore children. But *you* don't. Emily told me."

Emily groaned aloud. Me and my big mouth! she despaired, unconsciously shredding the flowers in her lap. "Now, now, Lady Georgiana," she protested feebly, "I never really said—"

Lady Georgiana, her full bottom lip thrust out petulantly, swiftly cut her cousin off by saying, "Yes, you did so, Emmy, just before. Don't you remember? You said Lord Edward hated the country and didn't like children, not even above half. I remember it most distinctly. I'm not completely stupid, you know."

"I see," Lord Edward drawled, looking at Emily appraisingly. Yes, the love of his life was clearly up to no good. Intelligent she might be, but she certainly wasn't his match in subterfuge. "My goodness, anyone would think you were warning your dear cousin off me—as if I were totally unsuitable. Wouldn't they, Miss Howland?"

Emily decided to attack, knowing her only other option was either abject apology or ignominious retreat. She wouldn't give the dratted man that satisfaction! "They most certainly might, my lord," she averred, lifting her bowed head to glare straight into his mocking green eyes. "But, as they say, if the slipper fits—"

"Oh, ho, Ned! If the slipper fits!" Lord Henry

crowed, liking the dowdy Miss Howland more and more. It wasn't that he disliked Lord Edward, whom he had known for dog's years. Indeed, he liked him immensely. But his friend had made that nasty remark about his grays. "Trumped your ace quite neatly, Ned, didn't she?"

Lord Edward leaned his head back to look up at his friend. "Enjoying yourself, Monty, are you—believing you've found yourself an ally, someone else who shares your low opinion of my character? Perhaps the two of you would like to retire now to compose a couplet or two intended to inform the rest of the world of my shortcomings?"

"I may be wrong, Cousin, but I think Lord Edward might be just the teeniest bit angry about something," Lady Georgiana whispered rather loudly into Emily's ear, causing the latter lady to immediately long for nothing more than a convenient bottomless pit into which she could hurl her embarrassed self.

When Emily didn't answer, Lady Georgiana leaned across her and artlessly repeated this observation to her childhood friend, Lord Delbert, adding innocently: "Poor Lord Edward. But I think Emily may have misjudged him, don't you? It's just that she's worried I might allow him to compromise me, you understand— Emmy seems to know *all about* being compromised, and—"

"Georgy, you clunch!" Emily fairly screeched, causing nearby heads to turn in the direction of

the small gathering. "I mean," she continued, her voice considerably hushed, "please, Lady Georgiana, I do believe this conversation has run its course. Why don't you and Lord Delbert take a stroll? Perhaps you can locate the juggler again."

Instantly diverted, Lady Georgiana hopped to her feet, clapping her hands in delight. "Oh, Emmy, that would be beyond everything wonderful! He said he'd teach me how he keeps those three pretty striped balls in the air at the same time. Come, Del," she ordered, holding out her hand. "Emily says you can come too."

Lord Henry Montgomery wasn't the most swift of persons, as application to his despairing papa would reveal, but he did see that his presence beside the blanket was clearly not required. Miss Howland was too embarrassed to so much as glance in his direction, but Ned—whom Monty had always said to have the most *speaking* eyes—was being silently eloquent in his wish to see both his friends gone.

Dislodging himself from his kneeling position beneath the tree, Lord Henry muttered something to do with gaining himself a firsthand observation of the swans swimming in the small stream in order to capture their haughty beauty in a poem he was working on, and slunk his thin, lanky self off, belatedly wondering if Miss Howland would thank him for his defection.

Miss Howland was, as a matter of fact, thinking some very unlovely thoughts about the man— one of the few people she had met in London whom she had hitherto believed to be her friend—while watching him as he departed, her head tilted as she mentally sketched a bushy squirrel tail tucked between his cowardly legs. Then, no longer able to ignore Lord Edward's penetrating gaze on her, she turned her head and began a minute inspection of the woven texture of the blanket, almost as if she were considering weaving one herself.

She'd cheerfully throttle me, Lord Edward observed, noticing the way the sun filtered through the overhanging branches, to dance on Emily's hair, bringing out surprising reddish highlights. Not that I can blame her, I guess, he added consideringly, remembering his impulsive, exploratory kiss of the other evening. Even now he found it difficult to believe he had actually dared to hold this intriguing woman in his arms, press his lips to hers, feel her tautly held body against his own.

He must have been the worse for drink, he decided, trying to understand how he had allowed himself to rush his fences that way. As he had known instinctively from the first, as he had explained to a condemning Burton, Miss Emily Howland required careful handling if he was ever to convince her he was sincere in his affection for her. It was clear to him that she considered herself out of the marriage stakes, neither beautiful enough nor wealthy enough to attract a suitor of his standing. For now it was enough that he had her interest, even if she didn't spare his feelings in letting him know how much she disliked him. Once they were down at Lyndhurst Hall, once she had gotten used to Reggie, then he would tell her what was in his heart. Only then could she believe he was sincere in his affections.

When the silence between them had stretched past the point of uncomfortable and entered into the realm of the absurd, he gathered up his courage and spoke. "I must apologize most profusely for the other evening, Miss Howland," he said airily, his carefully unrepentant tone causing her head to lift proudly. "I can't for the life of me imagine what possessed me to attempt such a thing."

"Is the word 'spite' not then in your vocabulary, my lord?" Emily's shoulders were stiff and straight as she looked down at him, and she felt a small surge of satisfaction as his gaze slid away from hers. "However, now that you are apologizing in earnest—if such a lame attempt can be thus labeled—perhaps you could exert yourself yet again and secure my wholehearted forgiveness by agreeing to cease and desist your pursuit of my cousin. Contrary to what you said that night, you still appear to be very much in the chase."

"That still rankles, does it?" Lord Edward drew himself up to a sitting position, wrapping his arms about his knees. "So much so, in fact, that you have been busily filling the little dear's head with all sorts of dire warnings about me. Isn't that right, Miss Howland?"

Emily destroyed yet another innocent daisy. "Yes," she admitted through clenched teeth.

"Did you tell her I eat little children for breakfast, by any chance?" Lord Edward pushed on, clearly enjoying himself. "Lady Georgy seems convinced I detest the little dears."

"I did no such thing!" Emily was stung into admitting. "I merely pointed out to her that if she were so witless as to marry you, she could not live at Chilworth Manor or raise her children there. The rest of it . . ." She faltered for a second or two, then went on, "Well, the rest of it just naturally *followed* somehow, that's all."

"Indeed?"

The ramrod-stiff spine straightened yet another degree. "Yes, *indeed*, my lord, and I'm not sorry!" she declared vehemently. "I'd do it again. Lady Georgiana deserves better than you. *Anybody* does."

Lord Edward reached up his index finger and thoughtfully scratched at his lean, tanned cheek. "Even you, Miss Howland? Even you? Methinks, ma'am," he said at last, "the lady doth protest too much. Are you sure you couldn't be just the tiniest bit *jealous* of Lady Georgiana? I am said to be damned handsome, and most eligible. You could do a lot worse, you know. And, truth to tell, I do believe I could be brought to like you, in spite of yourself."

"You conceited buffoon—you utter *monster!*" Emily gritted out the words, scrambling to her feet. "How dare you even suggest such a thing? Sir, I find you beneath contempt. Now, please leave me, or else I shall take myself off. I find I cannot be within twenty feet of you without longing to slap that silly grin from your too-handsome face."

Lord Edward, now also standing, tipped his head to one side and grinned even wider. "So, you spurn me, Miss Howland? You do realize, of course, that this means war?" he purred, sliding his hands into his pockets as if to show how little he feared physical attack.

"Meaning?" Emily asked, hating herself for needing to hear him say what she was sure he would say.

"Meaning, Miss Emily Howland, that I do believe I shall make Lady Georgiana my personal project from now on, just because it appears to bother you so. After all, I shouldn't like her to lose any sleep believing me to be the worst beast in nature, should I? I much prefer her to be madly in love with me. Old Horry is half in love with me herself—whenever I remind her exactly who I am—so I doubt I shall find much resistance on that front. I might even go so far as to make *you* fall in love with me yourself. Wouldn't that be a coup? Yes, I think I should like you to be in love with me, Miss Howland. Good day."

Emily's mouth opened and closed several times—fishlike, she thought wretchedly—as she struggled to find something damning to say in rebuttal before he bowed politely and bid her farewell, once more leaving her with nothing but her own fury for company.

7

⚜

For the next three weeks—twenty-one truly forgettable days and a like number of frustrating nights—Emily Howland fretted and seethed, powerless to thwart Lord Edward's determined assault on Lady Georgiana's heart, dreading the moment she would be called to her aunt's boudoir to be informed of her cousin's betrothal to the dastardly lord.

Nothing she said to the contrary—and Emily had tried everything from threats to downright pleading—could convince her cousin that Lord Edward was anything but "the sweetest man in the whole, entire world," especially (drat the man for being so underhanded anyhow, and may a pestilence infest all his houses) when he was behaving just as he ought—bringing flowers, complimenting Lady Georgiana on her gowns, and spending his every moment running tame in the mansion in Portman Square just as if he had a right to be there.

If Emily had truly believed her cousin's emotions to be seriously engaged, she would have days earlier thrown convention to the four winds and belted the smiling Lord Edward square in the chops (an unladylike action, but no more than he deserved), but she knew Lady Georgiana was too flighty to have really developed more than a passing interest in his lordship. She was still more than happy to accept the advances of her many other admirers, for one thing, and she still spoke of Chilworth Manor with more passion than she ever did of one Lord Edward Laurence.

The strangest thing was that Emily was fairly certain Lord Edward was also aware of Lady Georgiana's unconsciously fickle, immature nature. Not only was he aware of it, but it seemed to amuse him, which was just one more reason Emily longed to do the man an injury. He was clearly enjoying himself with this supposedly passionate pursuit, and she was becoming more and more convinced that he was doing it solely to infuriate her. But one never knew, did one? Betrothals had been accomplished on much less than Lord Edward's twisted form of courtship.

Tongues were beginning to wag, and more than once Emily had found herself on the receiving end of lectures given by condescending dowagers who questioned her chaperonage of her cousin. "Trotting a bit hard, ain't she?" one beplumed old harridan had suggested just last night, leering at Emily over the rim of her *fourth* full glass of wine—Emily, feeling mean but justified, had been counting.

But even worse than the scoldings of the old biddies were the endless hours Emily had to spend in Lord Edward's company, for, somewhat like Ruth, whither Lady Georgiana went, Emily was destined to go also.

When she could stand his teasing glances and veiled innuendos in silence no longer, she knew she had to do something so that she could be rid of him once and for all. And so, the morning after Lady Rutherford's ball—the one during which Lady Georgiana had stood up for no less than two waltzes with Lord Edward, *besides* going down to dinner with him!—she acted.

Scratching timidly at the door to her aunt's bedchamber, Emily obeyed the command to enter and spied out the dowager duchess sitting propped up against the carved backboard of her immense high bed, her graying head swathed in a ludicrously oversize lace-edged nightcap that had dropped down to cover one eye.

"Oh, good morning, my dear," her grace chirped, pushing back the nightcap and peering myopically at her niece, plainly trying to place the child. Her visitor looked so drab, yet somehow exotic, like a strange, foreign flower wilting from the shock of being transplanted into English soil. "We're having some tea, I believe. Um, shall I have, um er ..."

"Simmons, your grace," the middle-aged maid said, prompting her employer automatically as she entered the room and went to draw open the heavy velvet curtains, letting in the morning sun.

"Simmons—yes, of course. I knew that," the dowager duchess concluded happily. "Shall I have Simmons ring for some tea for you as well? It's quite good, you know. Really sets one up for the day, although I do believe I much prefer my chocolate. But I do believe I particularly asked for tea this morning. I wonder why?"

"To settle your stomach, ma'am," Simmons reminded her mistress, wondering yet again if she had enough money put by to move in with her sister in Liverpool for a restorative space. This latest job was beginning to wear on her nerves, even if her grace was the highest title she had ever worked for since coming to London. "I believe you told me you felt a bit queasy."

"I did? Oh, yes, I remember now. It was that horrid meal I had last night, wasn't it? Now, what was that—"

"River eel in parsley sauce, ma'am, a most unfortunate choice, I believe," Simmons said on a sigh, shaking her head at Emily, who was beginning to have second thoughts about her plan to use the duchess to thwart the romance between Lord Edward and her cousin Georgiana. "Shall I ring for another cup, miss?"

"Thank you, no, Simmons, I've already had my breakfast," Emily demurred, trying to convey her sympathy to the older woman with an understanding smile. "I just wish a few moments alone with my aunt, if you don't mind. I have something rather important to discuss with her, as I need her opinion."

Simmons returned the smile, sniffing her

amusement. "Good luck to you, then, ducky,"
she whispered, picking up some bits of discarded
finery and leaving through a small door cut into
the far corner of the large, overheated room.

"You have a problem to discuss with me, er,
um, my dear?" the duchess asked, wishing she
could remember the dear girl's name. Emma,
Ethel—it was something like that. "Please don't
tell me you wish to return to your home, wher-
ever that is. We're so close to settling Georgy. I
think Archy's boy is quite near the sticking point,
don't you? Such a nice young man—although he
doesn't hold a patch on his father, of course.
What's his name again?"

"Lord Edward Laurence, ma'am," Emily informed her aunt, sighing. Now she knew for
certain that it was not just her imagination running amok. After all, if Aunt Hortense had noticed it, surely the situation was serious. Deter-
minedly ignoring the curious pain she felt in the
region of her heart when she thought of Lord
Edward and Lady Georgiana bound together in
matrimony, she pushed on, "I must tell you,
dearest aunt, that I cannot in all good conscience
say that I approve of the match."

The duchess was immediately crestfallen, having already mentally packed her baggage for a
remove to Sussex and some longed-for peace
and quiet. "Why?" was all she found herself
able to ask, looking at her strange young niece
suspiciously, feeling the child to be responsible
for her sudden unhappy shift in mood.

"He's only a younger son," Emily substituted

wildly, still hoping she might be spared from revealing the entire sordid story she had—if needs must—decided upon.

"Oh, pooh," the dowager sniffed, waving her right hand, already adorned with three rings, which she considered ample jewelry for the morning hours. "As if that means anything. He's plump enough in the pocket," she informed her niece, for, although she might not be the most intelligent woman in the kingdom, she certainly knew well enough to make sure she was not handing her youngest child over to some penniless fortune hunter who would be forever sticking his legs beneath *her* dinner table!

I should have known, Emily berated herself, having already been subjected to her aunt's feelings on the subject of money. Hadn't she told her—with a noticeable absence of her usual empty-headedness—that it was pointless to put down a load of blunt purchasing a wardrobe for Emily to replace the sadly inadequate one she had brought with her from Surrey, saying that nobody would notice her anyway, once Lady Georgiana was in the room? Not that she was entirely stingy, for she had suggested Emily avail herself of some of her cousin's castoffs—which would have been wonderful to see, for Lady Georgiana was a good half-foot shorter and definitely less amply endowed than her cousin.

"He's also known to be a sad runabout," Emily offered weakly as her second complaint, hoping this line of attack might fare better than the first. "They call him Naughty Ned, you know. He's been said to do the most shocking things."

But, just as Emily had feared, this information seemed to thrill the duchess, who proceeded to relate to her niece a long, rambling story of Lord Edward's late father that served to put his son's feeble attempts at mischief to the blush— the details having something to do with a secret wager, a brewer's buxom daughter, and some visiting foreign minister with a penchant for lower-class females, although her grace's rendition of the escapade ended lamely, as the woman had quite forgotten the ending.

Emily swallowed hard, now knowing that she had no recourse but to tell her aunt what had transpired on the balcony almost four weeks previously. Going over to sit down beside the dowager on the edge of the bed, she laid her head in the woman's lap and whispered in what she hoped were strangled tones: "I fear I must tell you. Lord Edward ... he took ... he took advantage of me ... on the balcony ... last month ... at ... at Georgy's come-out ball, ma'am. I'm ... I'm *so* ashamed."

The dowager automatically reached out a hand to stroke the girl's head. "He kissed you?" she asked at last, finding it hard to understand that anyone, once he had clapped eyes on her beauteous youngest daughter, could conceive of doing anything so foolish. "Are ... are you *quite* sure of that, my dear?"

Emily's shoulders shook as if she were holding back her tears with some effort as she nodded furiously, biting on a small corner of the pink satin coverlet against the sudden rush of anger she felt at the patently incredulous tone of her aunt's voice. This was just one more insult to add to the budget of grievances she held against the insufferable Lord Edward. "Yes, ma'am—quite," she said. "He kissed me, and then he ... he ... Oh, I can't go on!" Why should she go on? It would totally destroy Emily's story if she told her aunt how Lord Edward had then gone on to insult her.

"Perhaps he was drunk. *That* would explain it," the dowager, still unable to believe she had heard aright, mused aloud, causing Emily to grind her teeth in outrage. "Oh, well, it was just a few kisses, wasn't it? The less said, the soonest mended, isn't that right?"

Emily sat up and glared angrily into her aunt's accepting face, stung to the quick. Obviously it didn't matter one way or the other if Lord Edward had dragged her into the dark and ruthlessly kissed her, just as long as—heaven forbid! —we don't *talk* about it.

"Oh, really, Aunt?" she heard herself saying through the strange hollow buzzing in her ears. "And if you were to return me to my mother—to your sweet sister, 'what's-her-name'—heavy and swollen with child, what would you do about that, *hmm*? Send along a polite note of apology, perhaps? Well, isn't that above everything wonderful? Good day to you, Aunt. I am *so* sorry to have bothered you!"

"Heavy and swollen with ... *Oh, dear!* Oh,

my goodness!" the dowager exclaimed in shock as she watched Emily flounce out of the room. "Maid! *Maid!* Oh, drat it all, what *is* your name? Come here at once! I need my vinaigrette!"

Lady Georgiana, shed of her constant companion for the evening, thanks to the very real headache Emily had contracted during her morning visit with the dowager, was enjoying herself mightily at Lady Agatha Winston's select party, flirting to her heart's content with her many suitors. She liked Lord Edward, liked him immensely, but she was glad he was absent this evening, as his presence seemed to keep all the other young gentlemen away.

Her mother, who was known to keep a loose hand on the reins at the best of times, was not paying too much attention to her daughter, being otherwise occupied, still trying to conjure up a mental picture of the handsome Lord Edward and the dowdy Emily Howland in anything even vaguely resembling a compromising position.

And so it was that Lady Georgiana, whose kind heart so easily overruled her lamentably soft head, allowed herself to be directed to a curtained alcove located on one side of the wide first-floor hall of Lady Winston's Grosvenor Square mansion.

Mr. Alastair Gresham, the young man who had succeeded in luring Lady Georgiana out of the main saloon, spent only a few moments cursorily inspecting the bust of Julius Caesar that occupied a pedestal in the alcove, explaining the sculpture's artistic and historic merits in such an obscure way that Lady Georgiana was convinced that her previous disregard for things ancient had been amply justified.

"Oh, Mr. Gresham, please don't continue, I beg you," she pleaded, pressing one small white hand to her forehead. "You said you had something of the greatest import to tell me, else I would not have accompanied you to this spot." Her pretty pink lips forming an attractive pout, she lamented, "And here I thought you were going to read me another poem. I particularly liked the one you read me last week, even if Emily did say that comparing my eyes to emeralds wasn't quite nice; as emeralds are so hard, you know, and they're stones too. Do you really think my eyes are like stones, Mr. Gresham?"

Mr. Gresham, far from being insulted—for he had paid only a paltry sum for the poem, to a struggling scribbler he'd chanced to encounter in one of the watering holes at the bottom end of St. James's Street—concentrated instead on the full lower lip Lady Georgiana displayed so artlessly, wetting his own lips in anticipation of his next move. He might not have a feather to fly with, which was why he was well known in society as one of the greatest fortune chasers in the *ton*, but seducing the beauteous Lady Georgiana held more than monetary reward as a lure.

Noticing Mr. Gresham's concentration on her face, as well as the rather aggressive stance he had assumed—a stance that effectively placed her with her back uncomfortably pressed into one corner of the alcove, away from the curtained exit to the foyer—Lady Georgiana belatedly realized her dangerous position and looked around for some means of rescue.

"Oh, my dearest Lady Georgiana," the hopeful swain crooned, his lips dangerously close to her ear, "how long I have dreamed of being with you like this. You are never alone, what with the proprietary Miss Howland always so close by your side, trying her best to discourage me. I cannot but view this moment as a golden opportunity, a happy circumstance that allows me to press my—"

"That you, Georgy? Deuced silly place for a person to stand in, ain't it?"

"*Del!* Oh, thank heavens!" Lady Georgiana shrieked gratefully, pushing the ridiculously ardent Mr. Gresham against the nearby pedestal so firmly that the unhappy man found himself clutching the heavy marble Caesar to his chest, else the bust would have toppled to the floor. "Please, Del, take me away from here."

Lord Delbert Updegrove might not have possessed the quickest brain in Mayfair, but he did have a fair understanding of this particular situation. Walking straight up to Mr. Gresham—not stopping until one foot was firmly planted atop one of the man's toes—he drew his fiery red brows together, glowered down menacingly upon the smaller man, and growled, "I believe I've never liked you above half, Alastair, you know that?"

Holding the bust protectively in front of him,

Mr. Gresham, wincing slightly, carefully eased his foot out from beneath his lordship's shoe, apologized for having been so inconsiderate as to have put it there in the first place, and hastened away down the hall.

"Where's Miss Howland?" Lord Delbert inquired archly, leaning one muscular shoulder against the wall, so that Lady Georgiana once more found herself effectively cut off from the hall, not that she believed her friend Del posed any threat to her. "I swear, Georgy, you're always in some scrape or another. Don't you pay any heed at all to what Miss Howland tells you? Maybe she ought to keep you on a leash."

Tipping her head to one side, her bottom lip thrust out angrily as she took exception to the general impression that she needed a keeper, she said, "Emily's home with the headache, or so she says anyway. Personally, I think she's pining away with love for your friend Lord Edward. Mama thinks so too."

"Oh?" Lord Delbert, conjuring up a mental picture of Emily Howland, could hardly conceal his astonishment or his curiosity.

Lady Georgiana didn't really believe what she was saying to be the truth—even if her mama had just today been asking some rather pointed questions about Emily and his lordship, and waxing poetic about babies and such, although that meant even less to her daughter—but she was just put out enough about being made to appear brainless beside her capable cousin to say something childishly spiteful.

"Then it's true?" Lord Delbert, who had just remembered Lord Edward's confession of a few weeks ago, shook his head, clearly concerned for both his friend and Miss Howland. "Who would have thought it? Sits it serious, then?"

Busily inspecting the hem of her new gown, which seemed to have somehow suffered some minor damage on the dance floor earlier, Lady Georgiana had to think a moment before she could reply to Lord Delbert's question. Was what true? What *was* Del talking about? Taking refuge in a show of temper, she returned smartly, "Are you calling me a fibber, Delbert?"

"My God," his lordship marveled, almost to himself. "I can't say as how I understand it, but if he did it, he did it, right? He *said* he did it, but I didn't really believe him. He was four parts drunk at the time, I'm sure, not that that's any excuse. No accounting for tastes, is there?"

"If who did what?"

"If Ned pulled Miss Howland off into the bushes, of course," Lord Updegrove returned hotly, unconsciously slipping into rather loose speech, but then he felt himself to be justified, as Lady Georgiana's confirmation had served to put him under some stress. "He said he did, but I thought it was the bottle talking. What are *you* talking about? You can't know anything about Lord Edward."

Now, everyone knows for a fact that bottles don't talk. Lady Georgiana certainly knew it, and she was beginning to feel rather smug. Obviously Lord Delbert Updegrove, for all his fine airs of being such a smartypuss, didn't have a clear understanding of the situation, whatever the situation was. Did he think she didn't know anything? Well, maybe it was time to show Del that she did so know a thing or two about Lord Edward! Raising her softly rounded chin, she declared importantly, if not exactly prudently: "A lot you know, Delbert Updegrove. *Everyone* knows that Lord Edward simply can't abide children. Emily told me herself. She was quite upset about it, actually. So there!"

"Ned . . . Miss Howland . . . *children! Oh, my God!*"

8

"Lord Delbert told me you weren't at Lady Winston's last night, Miss Howland." Lord Edward's tone was carefully neutral as he idly watched Lord Henry Montgomery and Lady Georgiana walk ahead of them down a tree-lined path in the park, sparing a moment to silently congratulate himself yet again that he had ingeniously maneuvered it so that he, rather than Monty, was walking with Emily. "I can only hope that you were not ill."

"I had the headache," Emily admitted shortly, uncomfortably aware of the curious tingle that persisted in her hand as it lay on Lord Edward's arm. She had another headache now, as a matter of fact, brought on by her cousin's offhand question over breakfast. "Can you help me, Emmy? What does it mean—to be pulled off into the bushes?" Lady Georgiana had asked, causing Emily to choke on her buttered toast.

"I have not the slightest idea, and you shouldn't say such things!" she had been stung into retorting, a response that had set her cousin to shaking her head sadly and mumbling something that sounded very much like "Del was right. You poor, dear thing."

Emily and Lord Edward continued their walk in silence for a few minutes, not knowing that, just a few yards in front of them, Lord Henry was listening intently as Lady Georgiana told him all about what she and Lord Delbert had learned about headaches and bushes and children —and some people named Henrietta and Peregrine, although he decided that they weren't worth the dozens of questions he would need to ask to gain a full understanding of their part in things.

It was enough to hear that his friend Ned had compromised poor dear Miss Howland. Why, if the ladies weren't present—and if Ned weren't such a deuced good shot—he would turn around right now and go slap his face, challenging his friend on the field of honor. Besides, he remembered gratefully, he had left his gloves behind in the carriage. One can't challenge a man correctly without first pelting him about the face with one's glove; it just wasn't done.

He'd have to contain himself, even consider talking the whole thing over with Del, not that *that* muttonhead would have a penny's worth of sense to add to the conversation; but at least it would give him some badly needed time in which to decide what his course of action should be, what a man of honor and decency—and limited courage—would do.

For the moment, seeing that he could think of nothing else to do, Lord Henry suggested that Lady Georgiana take the whole of her tale to her mother, the dowager duchess, since that lady was, so far, privy to only parts of it. After all, Miss Howland was under her roof, her protection. The old girl wasn't too bright, but she had raised five daughters; surely she would know just what had to be done.

"Do you feel, as I am beginning to do, Miss Howland, that we are being ignored?" Lord Edward asked after several minutes of uncomfortable silence had passed between them, inclining his head toward the couple in front of them, their two heads now nearly pressed together as they whispered back and forth feverishly, and too quietly to be overheard. "Perhaps it's time we made our way back to the carriage and returned you ladies to Portman Square, just in case Monty is in the process of offering for Lady Georgiana. They wouldn't suit, you know, and I'd hate to see the poor fellow shattered."

"Are you jealous, then, my lord?" Emily countered, unsurprised to find herself feeling somewhat evil. This man consistently brought out the worst in her. "Or perhaps, as you have been all but living in my cousin's pocket these past weeks without declaring yourself, you are being a dog in the manger, not wanting Lady Georgiana for yourself but not wishing for her to develop a *tendre* for anyone else."

Lord Edward stopped in the middle of the path and turned, looking down at Emily, inspecting her face feature by feature with his intoxicating light green eyes. "And what would you think if I were to throw caution to the winds and tell you that I don't care two snaps who Lady Georgiana marries, that she could run off with her dancing master for all it matters to me? What would you do, I wonder, if I were to tell you that I am only wooing your cousin in order to be with you? That I am madly, passionately in love with *you*, Miss Howland, and my only wish is to make you my bride? What would you say to that, my most infuriating Miss Howland? Will you marry me?"

Emily looked up into his eyes unblinkingly, seeing the dancing bits of sunlight that always lived there, her heart slowly crumbling into little pieces at her feet. How could he do this to her? How could he be so mean as to taunt her this way? "I'd say, Lord Edward," she told him at last, her chin held high so that it would not wobble as her emotions fought to get the upper hand, "that you are absolutely the meanest, most unfeeling person upon this entire earth. I know who I am, my lord, and what I am, and I don't need your nasty remarks to bring home to me the true nature of my position. Now, if you will kindly release my arm, I would—"

Lord Edward cut her off with an abrupt shake of his blond head. "You don't believe it, do you, not a word of it? Actually, I expected some initial resistance," he admitted, aware that he was rambling, but then, he hadn't realized he was going to declare himself until he'd actually opened his mouth and heard the words come tumbling out, "which doesn't really explain my behavior since first I met you, I am sure, so I don't know why I'm so upset. But I don't understand your continued dislike of me, truly I don't. I just didn't see any other way to gain your . . . Oh, never mind. Even Burton says . . . But that's another story, isn't it? You know, Miss Howland, I'm not all that unlikable. Hostesses don't bar their doors to me. Why can't you accept me?"

"Accept you! *Accept you!*" Emily was stung into exploding, unfortunately just as Lady Georgiana and Lord Henry turned and walked back to within earshot. "Lord Edward, I wouldn't have you if you were served up on a solid gold *platter!*"

Lord Henry, nodding his balding head sagely, whispered to his companion, "I see what you mean. She won't have him, will she? Poor fellow. You have no choice but to tell the dowager everything. Something must be done, and at once!"

"Something" was done; something that made perfect sense to Lord Henry Montgomery, Lord Delbert Updegrove, Lady Georgiana, and the dowager Duchess of Chilworth—a thought that in itself must be considered frightening.

Three days after that leisurely stroll in the park, and without bothering to share her plan with either of the principals involved, the dowager's solution to the delicate problem was served up to all of Mayfair with their morning chocolate.

Miss Emily Honoria Howland of Surrey, currently in residence with her aunt, the dowager Duchess of Chilworth, and Lord Edward Mortimer Sinclair Laurence, brother of Reginald Laurence, Marquess of Lyndhurst, were to be married the first day of June.

Burton, standing in just the wrong place as his master, his mouth full of hot coffee, read the announcement in the *Times*, spent the remainder of the morning carefully sponging the resultant rash of brown stains out of the front of his new waistcoat and wishing that his master would have the goodness to stop giggling.

The news was received quite differently in Portman Square, as Emily merely replaced the newspaper beside her breakfast plate (refolded most precisely), rose to her feet, walked slowly and purposefully up the stairs to her room, and locked herself inside, not appearing again for the remainder of the day, no matter how long and loudly anyone pounded on her door.

9

"I'll kill her!"

This vehemently voiced pronouncement, accompanied as it was by Lord Edward's graphic visual demonstration of his intention—consisting as it did of holding his cupped hands out in front of his body and then viciously, and with heartfelt enjoyment, squeezing an imaginary neck—caused Lord Henry to insert a finger inside his collar and ease the cloth away from his neck as he swallowed with an audible gulp.

"I mean it, Monty. I've thought it over, and nothing else appeals to me quite so much. I'm going to kill her." That Lord Edward felt just the opposite, that he would truly love to kiss Old Horry smack on the mouth for her opportune, if misguided, assistance, he would keep to himself. After all, the way Del and Monty seemed to bruit every second word he said around town, Emily would see through his subterfuge in a second and he'd be back where he'd started—which, as he already knew, was a long, long way from getting Miss Emily Howland to Lyndhurst Hall, much less to the altar. He could only hope he was a convincing actor.

"Oh, I say, Ned, isn't that a little extreme? Nobody said you had to actually declare your undying *love* for Miss Howland, now, did they? All you have to do is marry her. Besides, Del said you were talking about setting up your nursery—just a few weeks ago, wasn't it?—although I must say neither Del nor I really believed you were serious. You certainly aren't the sort to lumber about with a mess of indecision, I'll say that for you. Oh, no, once you put your mind to do a thing, you just go right out and do it. What I can't understand is why you're so angry. It's not as if the poor dear did it on her own, after all."

Lord Henry's observations stopped Ned in midstrangle, just when he was beginning to enjoy himself. As he had told Burton earlier, he always thought he had a flair for theatrics. How like Monty to burst his little bubble by not understanding him. "Miss Howland? You dolt! Why would I murder her? Who did what on their own? It was Old Horry that sent that notice to the press yesterday. I checked. Miss Howland is as innocent as I am in this stupidity . . . this . . . this *insanity!*"

Lord Henry reached up one pale hand to scratch at his nonexistent chin. Would it be foolhardy to point out that no *innocent* miss would be about to present his friend with a "token of her affection"—just about mid-February, if his calculations were correct?

Would it be gentlemanly, considering the fact that he did rather like Miss Howland, to even remark aloud about her compromised position? To be exact, would it be worth *his* neck to so much as hint at the reason for the forthcoming nuptials, after observing firsthand the extremely foul mood his friend Ned was wallowing in at the moment?

In the end, Lord Henry decided that self-preservation had a lot to recommend itself, and compromised. "Miss Howland must be in alt," he remarked noncommittally, wondering if Ned and the lady would appreciate a poem in their honor as a wedding gift.

"Emily Howland detests the very ground I tread on," Lord Edward pointed out, wondering yet again what her reaction had been to the announcement.

"I guess, then, that a poem is out," Lord Henry mumbled into his cravat. "But you can't murder the dowager duchess. Such things just aren't *done*."

Why had the dowager inserted the notice? That small bit of information still eluded Lord Edward. Pacing the carpet of his small sitting room with his hands clenched behind his back, he mused, as if to himself, "Maybe Old Horry just got the names mixed up; yes, she could do that. She must have meant to say that Lady Georgiana and I are to be wed; at least that would have made some twisted sort of sense. No, nobody's that forgetful, not even the dowager. She remembers m'father well enough."

"She never remembers me," Lord Henry put in helpfully, reaching into the nearby candy dish and selecting a tempting comfit. His friend didn't look very well, not very well at all. He looked a bit pale, as if he'd spent a restless night. Lord Henry shook his head in sympathy, then reached for another confection.

Lord Edward stopped his pacing and directed his green-eyed gaze to a point slightly higher and to the left of his friend's head. "The duchess knows she's done something very, very naughty, though. She wouldn't let me past her butler all day yesterday, and I tried a half-dozen times or more to see her. The plague, indeed. It's a good thing she's forgetful, for the woman can't lie worth a tinker's damn. I need to speak with Emily without any more delay. What time is it?"

Lord Henry pushed one skinny leg out straight and levered his bony hips upward so that he could slip a hand into his tight watch pocket. "It's gone eleven," he mumbled around a mouthful of candy. "You going to try to breach the walls again today?"

Taking his hat and cape from Burton, who had appeared from the hallway just a moment earlier, as if anticipating his master's summons, Lord Edward slammed the curly-brimmed beaver down ruthlessly on his blond curls, saying, "Damn right I am, Monty. There's no telling the damage that old lady's already done. Now, stop stuffing your face and follow me."

"Me?" Lord Henry gulped, sinking back into

the soft cushions as if hoping he could hide behind them. What would happen to him once his friend figured out the whole of it? "Why would you want me to . . . that is, I really can't see the reasoning behind my . . . oh, well . . . *actually* . . . I'm promised to Del for luncheon and . . . Oh, Ned, do I *have* to?"

"You do," Lord Edward retorted, looking curiously at his friend out of the corners of his eyes. "If I recall correctly, you and Lady Georgiana were acting most peculiar the last time all four of us were together. Not only that, but last night Del was over here lecturing me about remembering I'm a gentleman and to do the gentlemanly thing, or some such drivel. He was fairly deep in his cups, as was I, so I'm not really sure of everything he said. I just know it wasn't at all like Del. To tell the truth, Monty, I'm beginning to scent a rat. You wouldn't know more about this thing than you're letting on, would you?"

"Who—me? Don't be ridiculous!" Lord Henry wished his voice didn't sound quite so high, or so shrill. Rising jauntily to his feet, he grabbed his own cloak and hat and made to follow his friend out of the room. "Why would anyone ever think I knew anything?"

"I certainly wouldn't, my lord," Burton assured him, straight-faced, bowing to the young man most respectfully as Lord Henry, looking confused, politely thanked him.

The dowager Duchess of Chilworth was experiencing a most uncomfortable morning. Truth be told, she had been feeling most sadly out of curl ever since the previous day, when her niece had locked the door to the best guest chamber, refusing to see or speak to anyone.

The girl had accepted the meals brought to her by the servants—at least the dowager could comfort herself with the fact that the ridiculous child wasn't about to starve herself into a decline, it would be so bad for the babe—but the old woman couldn't help but feel partially responsible for her niece's unhappy situation.

After all, the chit wouldn't be in such a predicament if she herself had taken her responsibility more carefully, watched over her sister's child more closely, monitored her movements so that just such a scandal as this wouldn't, couldn't have occurred. But the girl seemed so mature, so responsible, so levelheaded.

"And so uninspiringly plain." The duchess sighed aloud into the bottom of her empty teacup. "Who would have thought she would be in any danger of being compromised—and by that sweet boy! How could I have known? The blame shouldn't all be mine. Minerva should have told me the girl had round heels. Isn't it just like Minerva to foist her hot-blooded offspring on me!"

"Your grace?"

"What is it, um, er . . ."

"Simmons, your grace," the woman clarified wearily. "I'm afraid I couldn't hear what you just said."

The dowager shook her head so that her oversize white linen nightcap slipped to one side, showing her thinning gray hair to disadvantage. "I see nothing unusual in that. You weren't supposed to hear me, young woman. I was talking to myself!"

Simmons nodded, accepting this admission calmly. "Sorry, your grace, I should have known."

"Yes, you certainly should have!" Satisfied that although the rest of her world seemed to have somehow been turned upside down, the domestic situation was still firmly within her grasp, the duchess announced that she wished to rise, as she was expecting visitors. That handsome young man would be back today, she was sure, and this time she would see him. As her dear late husband the duke used to say, "There is no sense in delaying the eventful"—or something like that.

"And Miss Howland has expressed her desire to bid you a personal farewell before she departs, your grace," Simmons added neutrally, careful not to let her feelings color her voice. When it came to loyalty, Simmons knew full well upon which side her daily bread was buttered; but she also liked the sad-looking young miss, and was not averse to seeing the duchess get a little of her own back for landing the poor companion in such a bumblebath. Miss Howland was not happy, any fool with an eye in her head could see that, and the duchess was the cause of that unhappiness. Now Simmons looked forward to enjoying the old woman's discomfort.

She was not disappointed. "Departs? Departs

where?" The duchess, momentarily forgetting her advanced years, as well as the height of her thick mattress in relationship to the shortness of her legs, scrambled crablike to the side of the bed and slid bumpily down to the floor, stopping only to catch her breath and to pull her snagged nightgown back down below her hips.

"She plans to go running to Minerva! I can't have that, I just can't! Minerva's too mean; she'll do something awful to me, I just know it. She once bit me, you know. Nasty girl, and such big teeth. I have to get them safely bracketed first. You—whatever your name is," she screeched, pointing to Simmons, "don't just stand there looking at me. Fetch me my clothing at once."

It had been an unhappy twenty-four hours for Emily Howland, long hours during which she had alternately wept and ranted and cursed the fact that she had ever been born, if this was a sample of what the rest of her adult life held in store for her.

As she hid in her room, traveling the long, lonely road from blank shock, to horrified disbelief, to hideous embarrassment, to righteous indignation—even as she, in the small, dark hours of the morning, reached a minimal level of resigned acceptance—one recurring thought had circled round and round within her aching head: how much she loathed and abhorred one Lord Edward Laurence.

She didn't know how he had accomplished it, and she certainly wasn't about to attempt delving inside his twisted brain to try to understand precisely *why* he had done it, but she knew Lord Edward was at the bottom of the ludicrous engagement announcement that had, overnight, made her, Emily Howland, an unknown from nowhere, the laughingstock of all London.

He had meanly teased her by hinting that he might wish to marry her, even while his every action showed her that he couldn't really be serious, and she had made it clear to him that he left her totally unmoved. She knew she had angered him, perhaps even injured his silly pride, but she had never thought he could be so spiteful as to subject her to public humiliation this way. She knew what he was about, of course. He had inserted that notice in the papers just so that he could refute it, so that he and his low-life friends could go round the town having a snigger at her expense.

How he would crow about her supposed one-sided love of him, her starry-eyed infatuation that must have convinced her to make her dotty aunt believe that he, Lord Edward Mortimer Sinclair Laurence—rich, handsome, and heir to the Marquess of Lyndhurst—had actually offered for such a poor, sad specimen as herself.

Oh, he had done the deed, all right, but he had miscalculated badly if he thought she was going to stay around to applaud him in his juvenile triumph. At four that morning, having slept not a wink since retiring just before midnight, Emily had hopped from her bed and commenced packing her trunk for the return home. Lord

Edward would just have to do his crowing on his own, without his victim around to suffer the stares and whispers he had provoked.

Now, having bathed and dressed in her shabby brown traveling dress, Emily was on her way downstairs to bid her aunt and cousin a hasty farewell, just as Simmons, wearing a commiserating face Emily found to be most disheartening, came by to say that the dowager and Lady Georgiana were in the drawing room awaiting guests and wished her presence as soon as possible.

Emily had just reached the door to the drawing room when the knocker banged loudly and one of the footmen waiting on a bench at the side of the foyer jumped up to answer the summons. Eager to get her farewells over with before the visitors could be shown in, Emily fairly ran into the room, stopping only when she heard Lord Edward's velvet baritone behind her in the foyer.

"Lord Edward Laurence to see the dowager duchess and Miss Emily Howland, if you please," the voice commanded, sending an indignant flush flying into Emily's pale cheeks and the blood pounding in her ears so that she didn't hear him add, with quiet good humor: "And I don't mean to be fobbed off with any more of your nonsense about plagues."

10

The double doors to the drawing room closed with a loud bang before Emily turned the key in the lock, successfully barring the young lord's entrance. Whirling around to place her back against the doors, she then surveyed the room in front of her, startled to see the dowager, usually a most energetic woman, lying on the settee, Lady Georgiana kneeling on the carpet beside her, vinaigrette at the ready.

"Oh, dear," Emily exclaimed, "I didn't realize! How could I have been so stupid, so self-centered? This is just as embarrassing for you as it is for me, isn't it, Aunt? Please forgive me."

Lady Georgiana, looking as radiantly beautiful as usual in a muslin gown of soft lime green, rose gracefully to her feet and advanced on her cousin. "Don't alarm yourself, Emmy, dearest," she said in a most motherly fashion, taking her stunned relative gently by the arm and leading her to a nearby chair. "Mama has had to deal with just this sort of thing before, and we'll

103

come through famously now exactly as we did
then, never doubt it. Only, please, don't be upset. Would you like some macaroons? Henrietta
was most partial to them, as I recall."

"Henrietta?" Emily echoed hollowly. "Your
sister Henrietta? What does she have to do with
anything?"

"Oh, I remember now," the dowager groaned,
clutching her hands to her bosom. "So it was
Henrietta who did that. Henrietta and . . . Oh,
dear, I can't seem to remember his name. Tall,
isn't he? With depressing dishwater-blond hair?"

"Peregrine, Mama," Lady Georgiana provided
helpfully, having arranged a light woven blanket around Emily's knees before returning to
her mother's side.

Emily raised a hand to her forehead and
rubbed at it gently, trying to understand. She
knew Henrietta, of course. Her mother had told
her about all of the Chilworth brood, seeming to
delight in the fact that none of them was any
too bright. Henrietta was the one who had made
that unfortunate alliance with the third son of a
country squire. Were her aunt and cousin sug-
gesting that Emily's supposed betrothal was also
a misalliance—with the male and female roles
reversed, of course? It seemed likely—just the
sort of comparison her relatives might make.
But what did macaroons have to do with anything?

She voiced her question aloud: "Why macaroons?"

"I can't imagine," the dowager responded, shaking her head. "I much preferred onions in cream sauce myself. At least, I think I did. It's been so long, you know. Perhaps you could tell us just what it is you do crave, and Georgy can have Cook prepare it."

The soft rapping on the door was replaced by the heavy pounding of a stronger, more insistent fist. Clearly the footman had been pushed aside and Lord Edward had taken charge of announcing himself. If Emily had been unsure of her deduction, the sound of Lord Henry's shrill voice confirmed her fears. "Oh, here, here, Ned. That ain't seemly. You're going to knock it down if you keep hammering away like that. I don't think the ladies are receiving. Ned? Ned! Where are you going now?"

Turning her head so that she could follow the sound of Lord Edward's retreating footsteps, Emily suddenly realized his intent and bolted to her feet, running to close the door to the morning room that adjoined the drawing room and also faced onto the foyer, but she was too late. Her arms spread wide, one hand on each door, she was nearly knocked onto her back as the man she had been trying to avoid barreled into the room.

"You!"

This accusation, voiced by both of them at once, served to put an immediate period to any conversation concerning macaroons or onions in cream or anything else that might have entered the minds of the dowager and her daughter to the detriment of the major problem at hand. "Lord Edward!" Lady Georgiana gushed as Lord Henry, always polite, slid into the room behind his friend and rushed to help her rise. "Oh, Mama, look! Lord Edward's here."

Emily, who was at that moment glaring dangerously into her enemy's openly taunting green eyes, snapped back nastily, "Oh, Aunt Hortense, look! Cousin Emily's leaving." Turning smartly on her heels, she took three quick steps before a strong hand clamped down on her forearm, pulling her to an abrupt halt.

"Shame on you, Miss Howland," teased Lord Edward, although no one but Emily detected the faint hint of laughter in his voice. "Running away? Oh, yes, I saw the trunk in the foyer. I had thought you had more bottom than that, truly I did." He was glad to see her, he really was, but he couldn't help but feel angry to learn that she was preparing to flee London rather than see him again. Such an action certainly didn't bode well for a smooth-running engagement, to say nothing of the effect it had on his opinion of himself, which had been growing steadily lower ever since he'd met Miss Emily Howland.

Emily whirled about, her ample bosom heaving under the faded material of her gown. "You don't like that, do you? When you made your plans for my humiliation, you never counted on your victim fleeing the scene, did you? You wished me to remain, to feel each separate sting of the arrows you and the rest of London would launch in my direction. Well, so sorry to disappoint you, my lord. You'll just have to carry on without me. Enjoy yourself!"

Although Emily tugged mightily to free herself, Lord Edward wasn't about to let her go. "Oh, how like you, Miss Howland," he said heavily, his worst fears confirmed. She blamed him entirely. He must have been all about in his head to think the dowager's interference could be looked upon as a blessing in disguise. Very well then, he decided, if it was anger Emily Howland wanted, it was anger she was going to get. Far be it from him to disappoint a lady! "How very much in character you are. You've tried and found me guilty without so much as a hearing, haven't you? It never would occur to you that *I* am just as much a victim here as you are, would it? Well, then, go on, run away—run back to whatever damp, dreary part of England you hail from and raise dogs. See if I care. I've broad shoulders. I can ride out this scandal alone."

Emily stopped struggling and stood quite still, looking up into Lord Edward's handsome face. "Cats," she mumbled inanely. "I thought I'd raise cats. You ... you didn't insert the announcement? You knew nothing about it either?"

Now Lord Edward did smile, though not at Emily and not at all in a kindly manner, to her way of thinking. "How do you like that, Monty?"

he asked his friend. "Sharp as a tack is our Miss Howland, once you gain her attention." Looking back at the woman in front of him, he continued: "No, Miss Howland, I did *not* insert the notice. Also, *you* did not insert the notice. Now, whom do you suppose that leaves?"

"Mama, I think Lord Edward knows you did it," Lady Georgiana exclaimed with a sudden burst of insight, turning about to look at her mother. "*Mama!* Oh, my goodness, Emily, look! I do believe my dearest Mama has fainted!"

Lord Edward was maddeningly unconcerned, his mind busy with his own problem. "She won't fall far; she's already lying down."

Emily slowly shook her head back and forth, a small sneer on her full, unpainted lips. "So gallant. And how very like you, my lord," she commented before, with one last sharp tug, she succeeded in freeing herself from his grasp in order to minister to her aunt.

It took several minutes to rouse the dowager, although Lord Henry was naive enough to point out that the woman didn't look as if she had fainted—for didn't her eyelids flutter just then?— but after a time she opened her eyes slightly and murmured, "Where . . . where am I?"

"In muck straight up to your knees, that's where," Lord Edward informed her kindly from behind the settee, "but we'll let that pass for the moment, won't we? Please, madam, could you possibly explain what possessed you to insert a notice in the papers concerning the supposed betrothal between Miss Howland and myself? We are both positively agog with curiosity, aren't we, Miss Howland?"

"But it's so simple. Didn't Lord Henry explain everything? Or Lord Delbert?"

Suddenly Lady Georgiana was the center of attention as all heads moved in her direction at the conclusion of this innocent question. Her mother looked at her in gratitude, as she believed she'd catch cold attempting to feign another swoon, while Emily and Lord Edward gazed at her in confusion. Lord Henry merely glared an unspoken warning, his huge Adam's apple working nervously in his throat.

Lady Georgiana liked being the centerpiece in any room, had liked it ever since she had sung her first party piece for visiting relatives the Christmas she was seven, and she preened a bit, adjusting the ruffle on her bodice, oblivious of the growing tension in the room.

"Georgy?" Emily prompted at last, sensing that Lady Georgiana, her little question posed, had no intention of elaborating.

"What? Oh, I guess he didn't did he? Not Lord Delbert either? How strange." Rolling her eyes, she took a deep breath and looked to her mother for guidance. "Is it seemly that we say anything? I mean, there are gentlemen present."

The duchess frowned, taking her daughter's words into consideration, while the remainder of the people in the room held their collective breaths, waiting to finally hear something that would make some sense of the situation. At last the dowager opened her mouth to speak, and they all leaned toward her expectantly. "Who's Lord Henry? Do I know a Lord Delbert?"

"That tears it!" Lord Edward pounded his fist against the back of the settee in exasperation, startling the dowager into sitting up straight, hanging on to her wig for dear life. "You did it, you know you did it, and we could care less if Monty and Del are strangers to you or by-blows from long-ago lovers you've forgotten over the years. Now, damn it all, woman, we're waiting— *why did you do it?*"

The dowager's eyes rolled up into her head as she fainted back against the overstuffed cushions —and this time even Lord Henry believed she had truly passed into unconsciousness.

Lady Georgiana, taking her cue from her mama, and knowing a naughty swear word when she heard it, even if she didn't quite understand what a by-blow was, promptly sagged into Lord Henry's arms, which was a poor choice, really, for the man wasn't overly strong, and the two of them ended up tumbling slowly into a nearby chair, Lady Georgiana slumped on Lord Henry's bony lap.

Only Emily, who was made of sturdier stuff, was unmoved by this outburst. "Congratulations, my lord," was all she said, calmly surveying the carnage about them. "You have served to fell them all with one mighty blow. But wait. Lord Henry is still conscious—or at least I think so.

Perhaps I'm being charitable, or merely overly optimistic. Do you suppose you should pursue your line of questioning with him, seeing as how he can't escape? Shall I call for thumbscrews?"

Lord Edward, who was raised to be better than he was being at the moment, but who didn't much care at this point what anyone thought of him, barked, "Shut up!" at his beloved and then walked round the settee to confront his friend. "Well, Monty?"

Lord Henry was trapped and he knew it. Where was Del when he needed him? He had been there sure enough when they were discussing how best to handle the problem. He was probably down at Gentleman Jackson's, pounding some poor soul to flinders in order to work up an appetite for luncheon, that's where he was, and Lord Henry wished, not for the first time, that his own strengths were less cerebral and more physical, for Ned was looking exceedingly dangerous.

"It wasn't my idea, Ned," he squeaked at last, shifting Lady Georgiana's inert body a shade to the left. "She's heavier than she looks. It's those small bones—they hide a lot."

"Monty . . ."

"Yes, well, I don't see what all the fuss is about," Lord Henry continued, now using Lady Georgiana as a human shield, holding her ragdoll-limp form in front of him as Lord Edward advanced across the carpet, blood in his eyes.

"After all, you have to do the proper thing—right? I mean, you wouldn't want the child to be born on the wrong side of the blanket. The dowager has just made it official, considering you and Miss Howland wouldn't stop fighting with each other long enough to set a date yourselves. People can count, you know, and February is going to be here before you know it."

"Child? What child? Whose child? What in blue blazes are you talking about? Monty, have you been drinking?"

"Oh, dear," Emily murmured quietly, but not so quietly that Lord Edward didn't hear.

" 'Oh, dear,' what, Miss Howland? Don't tell me this idiot is making sense to you."

Emily's mind returned to the conversation she and her aunt had had in that woman's chambers, and her own outburst that had something to do with being sent home to her mother "heavy with child." From there it was only a short skip to the questions Lady Georgiana had asked about "tumbling into the bushes" and her cousin's concern that Lord Edward didn't care for children. The macaroons, however, were what tied all these random bits of information into one huge misunderstanding and topped it off with a huge red ribbon.

Turning to face Lord Edward, Emily lifted her eyebrows hopefully, pinned a bright smile on her face, and raised her shoulders up to within an inch of her ears. "They think I'm pregnant," she chirped with what she hoped was a show of supreme enjoyment for a huge joke. "Isn't that above everything silly?"

"Pregnant? You? Who'd have the nerve?" Lord Edward threw back his head and laughed aloud, his laughter continuing for exactly three and one half seconds—Emily counted—before cutting off abruptly as his head snapped forward and he exclaimed: "Pregnant! You! Me? Oh, my Lord—me! *That's not funny!*"

"No, it isn't, is it, my lord? It is also not possible," Emily pointed out quite unnecessarily, leaning over to help her cousin, now conscious once again—but still vague as to how she had come to be curled up in Lord Henry's lap—to her feet. "Georgy, darling, do you think you are up to answering a few teeny questions?"

Lady Georgiana brightened at once. "I love questions," she gushed, then frowned. "Will I know the answers?"

"Oh, good grief," Lord Edward muttered as he stood next to his "betrothed."

"Hush," Emily ordered through clenched teeth. "After all, if you hadn't been so foolish as to go chasing after Lady Georgiana just to spite me, we wouldn't be in this mess in the first place. Now, be quiet, or else she'll swoon again."

"Ah, of course," Lord Edward said, leaning down so that his whispered words were audible only to Emily. "My fault again. I knew it would get back to me. Enlighten me, please: do you have any names picked out for the little darling you'll be presenting me with in—what was that date again—February?"

Emily calmly swiveled her head in Lord Edward's direction, lowered her chin against her shoulder, raised her slanted brown eyes to look into his face, and enunciated slowly: "Shut ... up."

"You're not quarreling again, are you, Emily?" Lady Georgiana asked, looking as if she was about to cry. "Lord Henry and I heard you say in the park that you wouldn't have Lord Edward on a platter, but that's silly, isn't it, considering that you're getting married. You really shouldn't fight—it can't be good for the baby."

Having spoken her little piece, Lady Georgiana realized that although she had been standing there ever so long, nobody had as yet asked her a question. She decided to remedy this lapse. "Aren't you going to ask me any questions, Emmy? You said you were. I don't know an awful lot about babies, you understand, even if I am the youngest and all the others have just oodles of children. I saw our cat, Mindy, have kittens once, behind the barn. Will that help?"

That did it. Lord Edward, who had been moving back and forth between frustration and amusement ever since he had set foot inside the Chilworth drawing room, finally succumbed to the latter. Staggering over to the settee, he lifted the unconscious dowager's feet to one side, sat himself down, and then replaced her feet on his lap, patting the bony, stockinged ankles comfortingly. Then he laid his head back against the settee and laughed until tears streamed down his cheeks.

Emily stood alone in the middle of the room, her arms spread beseechingly, her mouth opening and closing like a landed salmon as she struggled to find her voice. Then, just as Lord Henry began leading the puzzled Lady Georgiana out of the room, the dowager roused, raised her head, looked around the room, and asked: "Would you like some onions in cream, my dear? You look a little queasy."

11

"I must say, Ned, you're taking this whole engagement business rather well, considering." Lord Delbert's compliment delivered, and obviously relieved that his friend Lord Edward had not already demanded satisfaction from either him or Lord Henry on the field of honor—after having read Lord Henry's hysterical missive (an uncharacteristically ungrammatical communication, not that its recipient would notice such a lapse), delivered an hour earlier to Gentleman Jackson's—he sank into a chair and allowed a deep sigh to escape his lips.

Lord Edward, his left arm draped negligently on the mantel, inclined his head in his friend's direction and gifted him with a rueful smile. "I hesitate to point out that it's just that sort of simplistic deduction that has created 'this engagement business,' Del," he reminded the man almost kindly. "I wouldn't wish to alarm you, old son, since you have yet to pick up on it on your own, but you have caught me in the midst of a bad moment. I have to decide precisely how I am going to handle things with Miss Howland so that she does not end up hating me. In the interim, I suggest you do yourself a large favor and button your lip so that I can think."

Lord Delbert digested this advice slowly—and badly. "But Monty's note says the gel ain't really increasing, that we all just thought so. You do still mean to marry her, don't you? I mean, it's only proper. Is her family battening on you already? Pity. It was only a bit of frolic you were having, after all. Unless ... Good God, Ned, the girl *was* willing, wasn't she? If you ask me, she should have been demmed grateful, considering she's without funds and totally ineligible, though it still puzzles me what you ever saw in the female to drag her into the bushes in the first place. Three parts cast away, were you?"

Once again, as it seemed to have become his custom in these last few days, Lord Edward became quite angry. Angry that Lord Delbert couldn't see Emily the way he did, angry that his friend thought he'd care a snap whether or not his bride came to him with her pockets well-lined, and even angrier that anyone would think his beloved was so loose as to topple backward into the bushes with a man she proposed to detest. *"You idiot!"* he exploded, concentrating first on restoring Emily's good name. "What does it take to get through to you? Nothing happ—"

"No, he was not drunk," interrupted the subject of this debate from the doorway, where she had been standing unnoticed for some moments, "although you are not, alas, the first person to put forth that question. Good day, my lords. I am truly sorry to intrude upon you like this, unannounced, but—"

"Shame on me, Miss Howland," Lord Edward broke in, already moving across the room toward her, his green eyes flashing both a threat and a warning to the embarrassed Lord Delbert, "if I appear to doubt your sincerity in this instance, but—"

"—but that strange little man, most probably your butler, for I cannot quite see him in the role of bodyguard—seemed reluctant to alarm your gentler sensibilities by admitting an unaccompanied female," Emily pushed on doggedly, her nose raised, as if testing the air.

Lord Edward stopped midway across the carpet and pulled a wry face. "Even while fighting the very lowering feeling that my function at this moment is one of being relegated to nothing more than that of a minor character in a farce, destined to speak only lines meant to serve as verbal bridges over which the leading player can then tread, triumphant, I feel I must ask: What, then, did you *do* with the so-prudish Burton, Miss Howland, as you are, after all, here?"

Emily's eyelids lowered, hiding her expression as she mumbled something that sounded very much like "the cabinet under the stairs," before she went on more loudly: "While your abrupt departure from Portman Square this noon was not entirely without its small portion of personal appeal to me, my lord, I do believe you could have had something more to the point to say about our supposed upcoming nuptials than to say 'see you in church' as you took your leave.''

Lord Delbert's shocked gasp echoed softly in Lord Edward's snort of amusement.

"Therefore," Emily continued, refusing to be ruffled, "as my aunt and cousin have both re-tired to their rooms—doubtless to begin stitch-ing 'little things,' for I fear they have yet to let it sink into their vague skulls that I am *not* carry-ing your child—I took it upon myself to run you to ground so that we may settle this problem as quickly"—she spared a moment to look daggers at Lord Delbert, who was leaning forward in his chair, utterly enthralled—"and as *quietly* as possible."

Lord Edward shook his head. "And arriving on my doorstep unaccompanied in the middle of the day, Miss Howland—is that how you hope to silence all the wagging tongues in the *ton*? How comforting it is for me to have my reputa-tion resting in your clever hands."

"I see no reason for you to be so obnoxious, Lord Edward," Emily sniffed, her pale cheeks showing a faint hint of color.

"Yes, of course," he responded levelly, gestur-ing for Emily to take a seat even as he longed to pull her ugly dark green bonnet from her head. The first thing he'd do once they were married would be to burn every stitch she owned! "I have this lamentable tendency to overreact.

Please forgive me—and please excuse me for a moment while I effect poor Burton's rescue. The large storage cabinet, I believe you mumbled? I do hope you didn't squash his suit of clothes. He's very particular, you know, and I'd hate for him to take offense. After all, we may wish refreshments later."

Emily sat down primly on the edge of a small dusky blue divan and nodded to Lord Delbert, who had just gratefully subsided back into his own seat after standing at attention the moment she had entered the room. "You disapprove as well," she declared a trifle peevishly.

"Of locking old Burton under the stairs?" he deduced, furrowing his broad brow as he considered the question. "Can't say as it matters one way or the other to me, actually, although it must have been something to see. You're nearly twice his size . . . er, I mean . . . Why do you ask?"

Emily was not offended. It was true, after all: the butler was very small, most probably one of those dwarfs she had read about, and even if he was nearly as round as he was tall, she'd had no difficulty in grabbing the recalcitrant servant by the ear, as she was used to doing with her younger siblings, and depositing him inside the cabinet. "I was referring to my arriving here both unannounced and unaccompanied, my lord," she said mildly.

"Oh, yes, yes, of course," Lord Delbert said, embarrassed. "Surely it's not my place to pass judgment, Miss Howland. Is it?"

Emily tilted her head first this way, then that, considering. "I don't know, my lord. After all, such a piddling thing as it not being any of your concern certainly didn't stop you before—you or Lord Henry or my cousin. You all seem to have encountered little problem with your collective consciences while rushing to pass judgment on my supposed indiscretion with Lord Edward."

Lacking a suitable reply, and knowing the dratted female was well within her rights to take him to task—indeed, he was somewhat surprised she hadn't as yet conked him over the head with something heavy—Lord Delbert cravenly picked up two comfits from the always full candy dish and popped them into his mouth. After all, it was impolite to talk with his mouth full—and it seemed he had spoken more than enough already. Drat Georgy and her silly stories about babies—this entire mess should be laid at her door!

"Miss Howland?" Lord Edward reentered the room, his handsome face wearing an amused smile. "Burton sends both his regards and his congratulations—whether on our betrothal or your conquest over him in battle, I'm not quite sure—and wishes to know if you desire tea before you depart. He has also taken the liberty of sending one of the stable lads round to Portman Square to bring back a maid in Lady Chilworth's carriage. Good man, Burton, a real treasure, and he seems to have taken a liking to you. Something to do with 'gumption,' I believe. I was sure he would be all for sending you home in a hack—and sans the tea—but Burton is every inch the gentleman. We could learn from him, Del and I, if we chose."

"We don't choose, Ned, do we?" Lord Delbert was beginning to feel depressed.

"No, my friend," Lord Edward assured him gently, "we don't, although," he went on musingly, "we might wish to apply to Miss Howland here for some pointers in the manly art of defense. Tea?"

"I don't require any refreshments, my lord," Emily cut in, anxious to have this distasteful interview concluded as soon as possible. What an arrogant, overbearing ... Oh, what was the use? Emily bristled momentarily, and then relinquished her anger. After all, having anyone believe that she—plain, unprepossessing Emily Howland—had lured Lord Edward into a romantic indiscretion was highly flattering.

To Her. Definitely to her. But not to him. Not to Lord Edward Laurence, who had beautiful females dropping into his arms like ripe plums anytime he desired. No, for him the supposition that he had seduced her, along with the engagement announcement, could only be viewed as an unremitting disaster, with no positive aspects to lend it some small humor or palatability. Lord Edward had every right to be upset. Emily sighed. "Now, if you would be so good as to sit down, my lord, perhaps we may get on with the reason for my visit?"

"Good heavens, yes," Lord Edward agreed almost jovially, for, he was surprised to realize, he was actually enjoying himself. "I am, I assure you, all ears, if you have any suggestions to make to the point."

Emily barely repressed the urge to box his ears, her recent sympathy for her supposed *fiancé* evaporating as swiftly as it had come. Of course she had a suggestion! Did he think she had slunk out of Portman Square via the tradesmen's door, walked a depressing two blocks before locating a decrepit, *smelly* hack willing to bear up a solitary female, and opened herself up to Lord Edward's certain-to-be-voiced insults (and Lord Delbert's asinine remarks, although, to be fair, she hadn't given too much thought as to whether or not Lord Edward would be entertaining—a gentleman, that is—when she arrived), without there being a good reason for the visit?

"Well, Miss Howland?" Lord Edward prompted when Emily didn't answer.

Emily frowned, then tried to concentrate once more on the problem at hand. "We must have the duchess insist all the newspapers involved immediately print retractions, of course," she pronounced firmly, sure she was correct in her assessment of the situation, and wondering yet again why his lordship had not seen the obvious.

Lord Edward, who had been expecting just such a suggestion from her, immediately burst into speech. "Oh, yes, of course! Why, do you suppose, did I not think of that? Perhaps it was too simple—or just too bloody ridiculous! My God, woman, is it your desire then to make us even more the laughingstock than we already are? How do you propose to word the thing? 'Dear Readers—*whoops!* There seems to have been a small error . . .' " He turned to his friend. "Del! Can you just imagine that?"

Lord Delbert obediently squeezed his eyes shut and tried to picture the article as it would doubtless appear in the nastier columns. Then he grimaced. "You'll have to rusticate at Lyndhurst Hall, of course. For about two years, I'd say," he prophesied at last, opening his eyes to look gloomily at his friend. "And we were going to travel to Scotland together, too, you and Monty and I. We'll miss you, Ned."

"Oh, dear, please stop," Emily said scornfully, slanting her gaze toward Lord Edward, who was doing his best to look like a puppy that had just been unfairly kicked, "else I fear I shall cry." She then shook her head to let him know she wasn't having any of it.

Lord Edward stood up and moved back over to stand in front of the cold fireplace. She wasn't going to let this be easy, and he would be damned for the greatest fool in nature if he would allow this golden opportunity to slip away from him. "Perhaps, Del, if you would be so kind as to tell Miss Howland how you foresee *her* future if this retraction is printed?" he urged, trusting Del to be his usual tactless self.

Lord Delbert chewed on this question for a few moments, just long enough for Emily to begin to feel distinctly uncomfortable, then pronounced importantly: "I imagine society will have a good laugh at her expense and then . . . er . . . *forget her*. That's if she goes home straight-away, naturally, although I'm sure the stories will follow her for some months, even in . . . Where is it you live, Miss Howland?"

"Surrey," Emily rasped huskily, thinking of her mother, her brothers and sisters—the *neighbors*.

"And if she remains here?" Lord Edward prod-ded, watching Emily closely and knowing his friend's words had at last struck a nerve. He hated doing this to her, longed for nothing more than to gather her in his arms and kiss the pain away, but it was the only way the rest of his plan could work in its new, hastily amended form.

"If she stays out the Season here in London," Lord Delbert pushed on, gaining confidence, as he felt he had their full attention, "it will be much, much worse. Everyone and his lady wife will think she was the one who inserted the notice, you see."

"And why is that, Del?" Lord Edward asked, once again knowing the answer.

"Well, that's easy enough, Ned. I'm surprised you didn't see it for yourself. Because any fool would know that *you* of all people would never actually offer for an utter nobody, a . . . Oh, I say, Ned, I'm late for an appointment. I really must dash. Good day, Miss Howland," Lord Del-bert rushed on, already on his feet and moving toward the door, his normally ruddy complex-ion beet red with embarrassment and chagrin that Ned had trapped him into such a glaring *faux pas*. "It was so nice seeing you again; really it was."

"Lord Delbert," Emily choked out thinly, her head bowed as she pretended to examine the small garnet ring on her right hand, a gift from her mother and the best piece of jewelry she owned.

"I didn't want to do that, you know," Lord Edward said gently once they were alone, before, his heart going out to her, he blurted, "Oh, look here, Emily, can't you see that—"

"The young miss's carriage is without, my lord," Burton broke in repressively from the doorway, where he had been standing unnoticed for some minutes, hearing every word, understanding every motive—and therefore knowing that his master was about to confess all, thereby making a fine mess of everything.

"Go away, Burton," Lord Edward replied tersely, still concentrating on Emily's bent head.

"I'm a complete idiot, aren't I?" Emily said quietly after a long, uncomfortable silence, still twisting the cheap ring round and round her finger.

"*No!* It's all my—"

Burton, who had stayed in the doorway, for, after all, there was no other chaperon present now that Lord Delbert had cut and run—indeed, the servant was secretly surprised (and more than a little sorry) that the fellow had lasted as long as he had—pointedly cleared his throat and glared at his employer.

Lord Edward, who knew that particular look well enough from his younger days, sighed, and then inclined his head slightly in recognition of the unspoken command. As Burton had pointed out just this morning at breakfast, he still had to get Emily down to Lyndhurst Hall. The engagement announcement had played right into his hands, and he'd be seven kinds of a fool if he didn't take advantage of it. "Miss Howland," he said softly, pushing himself away from the mantel and going over to take her restlessly moving hands in his own, "I believe there is a way out of this thing for both of us—if you can find it in your heart to trust me."

Emily raised her head slowly, her deep brown eyes nearly black with pain. "Do I have any other choice? I'm listening, my lord."

12

It had been quite the most lowering experience in Emily's life. Even three hours later, and in the privacy of her comfortable room in Portman Square, her cheeks still burned with shame when she thought about it.

How could she have been so harebrained, so impetuous? Whatever had possessed her to ever consider running to Lord Edward for assistance? It was like running to a lion to be protected from a tiger. Had she really believed he held any answers for her—the man whose very perverseness had been the cause of all her problems in the first place?

Oh, yes, Emily mused, staring at herself in the ornate gilt-edged mirror hinged atop the dressing table—sparing only a moment to run a finger absently along the length of her nose and once again rue nature's decision to gift it with that slight bump just at the bridge—all the *real* blame could be laid squarely at his door.

She might have been willing to carry her share

of the burden of guilt for the rather ticklish consequences of everyone's mistaken notions, but it was Lord Edward who had invited this avalanche of disaster to come crashing down around their ears in the first place, him with his nasty taunts and totally reprehensible actions.

She would never have said a word to the duchess—not a single, solitary word—if *he* had not all but dared her to do something to rid Georgy and herself of his unwanted attentions. He had merely been frolicking—reveling in Emily's frustration—knowing all along his pursuit of her cousin, not to mention that ridiculous so-called proposal he had dared to tease Emily with herself, had not been serious.

In the first place, Emily had at last calmed herself enough to realize that if Lord Edward had *really* developed any sort of *tendre* for Georgy, he would have gone straight to her to clear himself, so that the object of his affections would not be obliged to view him in disgust—as any man who had fathered a child and then refused to wed the woman he had compromised must be seen.

Raising her hands to take the pins from her hair, Emily hesitated a moment, leaning forward to look herself in the eye. "Now, why do you suppose that one fact—set as it is amidst a rare bellyful of absolutely horrendous facts— serves to lift your spirits, Emily Howland? Don't tell me you actually have some feeling for that odious man?"

She stared at her reflection piercingly until

she was forced to divert her eyes from her candid inner self, and began ruthlessly pulling the pins from her hair. "Of course you don't! Don't be ridiculous!" she scoffed, knowing her tone wasn't quite convincing.

All the pins removed, she pushed her hands through the long, heavy mantle of hair and then shook her head vigorously, not realizing that the wild tangle of red-brown hair that now framed her face added a sultry hint of mystery to her slanted eyes while lending an unlooked-for air of wantonness to her generous lips and high cheekbones.

Rising to her feet, she opened the high front closing of her gown and let the garment drop to the floor, carefully averting her gaze from the mirror and the sight of what she considered her most embarrassing feature—her high, full bosom.

Bosoms were, she acknowledged, in vogue at the moment, but her seeming excess had been endlessly tut-tutted over by her nervous mama, who was a much less generously endowed and extremely modest female, causing Emily to believe that—as with her nose—nature had painted her with far too wide a brush.

To hide her "flaw," Emily had, since her early teens, worn her gowns long-sleeved and buttoned to the throat, favoring dark, drab colors that would call less attention to her unfortunate "gifts." The advent of the *empire* waistline, which so successfully concealed many a thick middle in others, completely hid the fact that Emily's waistline, in contrast to her breasts, was exquisitely infinitesimal.

Her hips, also generous, though not overly padded, were likewise forever shrouded in the heavy draperies she employed as camouflage, as were her long, straight legs. The resultant overall look of dowdy dumpiness that had caused Lord Edward some secret concern in fact concealed a figure that would have brought tears of joy to Botticelli's eyes.

But Emily, slipping a fresh, yet depressingly similar gown of muddy green—"the exact same shade as a moldy leaf," Lord Edward had commented *sotto voce* when first confronted with the gown—was blind to her unique, beautifully sculptured beauty, seeing only that she was "different," a fact that never showed to more personal disadvantage than when she was inevitably compared to her petite, finely featured, blond-haired cousin.

The dinner gong sounded jarringly just as she inserted the last restraining pin into the curled, upswept style that was so flattering to Lady Georgiana, while, alas, making Emily look much like she had a weather-beaten bird's nest stuck to the top of her head, and she took a deep breath, pushed back her shoulders, and turned for the door, determined to somehow get through what she was sure—thanks to the *enterprising* Lord Edward and his nefarious "Plan"—was destined to be the most difficult evening of her life.

They were all waiting for her when she came downstairs: her aunt, her cousin, and that dreadful, dreadful man. "Good evening, my dearest Emily," Lord Edward greeted her loudly, immediately moving across the wide drawing-room carpet to bow over her hand and kiss her fingers with a show of passion that may have convinced her relatives of his ardor but only left Emily feeling used. "May I say that you are looking well this evening?"

"Yes, she does have a little color tonight, doesn't she?" her grace agreed in some amazement as Lady Georgiana helped her to her feet in preparation for moving into the dining room. "Once the uncomfortableness of the morning was over, I always felt much more the thing for the rest of the day—at least I think so. But it doesn't last, my dear, you'll be happy to know, the queasiness, that is. Except with my third—or was it my second? I had a terrible time, even with the onions in cream, and we missed nearly the entire Season."

"Mama, Emmy says she's *not* increasing," Lady Georgiana whispered loudly. "Don't you remember? She just always looks sort of green."

"You know," Emily said offhandedly as she vainly tried to extract her hand from Lord Edward's grasp, "if I didn't know she was being sincere in her efforts to help me, I'd be tempted to box my dear cousin's ears."

Lord Edward hid a smile with his hand as he ushered Emily in to dinner. "At least she seems to have digested the fact that you're not carrying my child. Now, if we can only convince dear Old Horry—"

"Of course *you* can," Emily interrupted as he deliberately made a ceremony out of holding her chair. "I remember how convincingly you spoke this afternoon of accomplishing just such a daring breakthrough this evening. My only question is, if your plan works, what will you then do for an encore—flap your arms up and down and fly three times around the chandelier?"

"It might be easier," Lord Edward conceded before walking around the table to his own seat directly across from her, noting that the butler had already taken care of seating the duchess and Lady Georgiana.

As the first course was being served, her grace looked around the table, frowning. "We are such a small party, aren't we? I imagine I'll be expected to have some sort of do—with all sorts of people milling about, stuffing their faces and drinking the cellars dry. I wouldn't wish Minerva to think I wasn't doing the right thing for her dear daughter. Has a nasty disposition, Minerva—but then, she never was my favorite. What do you think, Lord . . . er . . . ?"

"Call me Ned, please, ma'am," Lord Edward supplied kindly, deciding his opinion of Emily's mother wasn't really required. "After all, we're soon to be family. Isn't that right, darling?"

Raising her eyes from her plate, Emily saw that Lord Edward was smiling at her in a way that set her toes to curling inside her slippers. So, this was it—the opening salvo of his lordship's brilliant Plan. She loathed it already. "Yes, er, yes . . . of course!" she stammered, outwardly smiling, inwardly seething.

"But, Emmy," Lady Georgiana broke in, obviously confused, "just last week you told me that you'd rather be dunked headfirst in pitch and hung out to dry in Piccadilly than allow yourself to be married to Lord Edward. She said it just last week, Mama, I'm sure she did. Didn't you just say that last week, Emmy?"

"Piccadilly?" Lord Edward repeated, looking at Emily in genuine amusement. "My goodness, darling, there are times you really do shock me. Now, be a good girl and tell your dear cousin the truth. After all, it was just a silly lovers' quarrel."

Step Two of the Plan, Emily acknowledged silently, wishing the dining table wasn't so wide that she couldn't deliver a sharp kick squarely on his lordship's shin. "That's right, Georgy. We had an argument, Lord . . . er . . . *Ned* and I, and I was just being mean." Turning to face her aunt, she continued just as Lord Edward had rehearsed her, and hating every moment of it: "We had already planned to announce our engagement before our spat—the one Georgy and Lord Henry overheard in the park. Naturally, when I saw the announcement in the paper, I was angry that Ned had gone ahead and inserted it without telling me. Imagine my surprise when we found out you had already guessed our secret—and we thought we had been so clever, hiding our attraction to each other. Actually, dearest aunt, we have you to thank for making us realize that we really do belong together."

"Me?" the duchess questioned, momentarily forgetting that she had been the one to insert the announcement in the first place. "Oh, yes—it was me, wasn't it? My goodness, sometimes I surprise myself." She blushed and waved her hand as if to diminish her own importance. "It was nothing, my dears, really. You don't have to thank me."

Lord Edward caught Emily's eye and winked his approval of her performance, so that she was tempted to stick her tongue out at him in a most childish way. "If you say so, ma'am, but I think you're being too modest. You can be sure we will always remember you as the person who brought us to this point ... er ... this happy conclusion. There is just ... well, just this one small niggling thing ..."

"Yes?" Hortense was leaning forward in her chair, eager to be of assistance. Nobody had ever asked for her help before, which seemed quite silly now, as she was proving to be so good at it.

"Yes," Lord Edward went on smoothly. "You see, Emily and I are having some problem with the June first date—the one you used in the announcement. As it is just a month away, I doubt we could possibly arrange everything to our satisfaction in so short a time, what with Emily's family being in Surrey, and my brother Reginald never coming to town, and, oh, just all sorts of knotty problems. Would it be all right with you if we postpone the wedding for a few months? Perhaps August would suit?"

"But . . . but . . ." The duchess looked from Emily to Ned and back again. "But . . . the *baby!*" The duchess might have been vague about other things, but when it came to indiscretions, she had a memory like an elephant.

Lady Georgiana laid down her fish fork with a resigned sigh and said, "Mama, Emmy isn't going to have a baby. Lord Edward only kissed her the once, and it wasn't in the bushes, it was only on the balcony. We were wrong, we were all wrong—Lord Henry, and Del, and you, and me—don't you remember?"

"Only one kiss? Not going to have a baby?" The duchess furrowed her brow, trying to get everything clear in her head. She didn't recall any Lord Henry—although the name Del seemed familiar—but she couldn't be expected to remember everything. "Well, then, why did I insert the notice if it wasn't to quash a scandal?"

"We wanted you to, ma'am," Lord Edward supplied quickly as he saw that Emily was about to open her mouth—undoubtedly to say something that would queer the whole Plan. "You were playing Cupid, ma'am, and may I be so bold as to say, you did a bang-up job of it. All of London is buzzing about it. It's just that the *date—*"

"Yes, yes, the date," Horry interrupted, very much in charge now that she understood the way of the thing. "Not increasing, huh? Well, doesn't that just beat the Dutch? This way we won't have a lot of old biddies sitting about counting on their fingers after you're married. A pity Henrietta wasn't so fortunate. Have you met her husband? I can't remember his name, but he's a dreadful, dreadful man. Dreadful child too, for that matter. Favors his father. No chin, none at all."

"Henrietta's baby is a girl, Mama," Lady Georgiana said punctiliously.

"A girl?" Hortense clucked her tongue. "It's even worse than I thought. Thank heaven I won't be the one to have the launching of her."

"The date, Aunt," Emily prodded, her fingers crossed in her lap. According to Lord Edward, everything depended on the date. If they could only get the duchess to postpone the wedding until after the Season, a discreetly worded notice in the newspapers sometime during the summer, telling of the termination of the engagement, would be no more than a nine-days' wonder.

Lord Edward had magnanimously allowed that Emily could be the one to cry off, once she was safely back in Surrey, and his plan to rusticate until the fall Little Season would silence the rest of the talk. It was a good plan, decidedly better than an immediate retraction, even if it did call for the two of them to pretend an engagement for the next month.

"August would be fine then, I suppose," the duchess pronounced at last, and Emily could hear Lord Edward's audible exhalation of the breath he must have been holding as he waited for her answer. "You'll write to your mother and, um, tell her that we, er . . ."

"Of course, Aunt. I'd be happy to!" Emily exclaimed, knowing the letter would never be written. News from London was spotty and delayed at best, and she planned to be home long before any word of her supposed engagement could reach her family's ears. "Mother will be so grateful to you, Aunt," she added for good measure.

Suddenly the duchess's watery blue eyes took on a haunted look. "Surely *I'm* not responsible for putting on the wedding. Am I?" Playing Cupid, obviously, was one thing. Paying for the privilege was another kettle of fish entirely, and infinitely less palatable.

"Of course not, ma'am," Lord Edward hastened to assure her. "We'll be married from Emily's home. Right after our trip down to Lyndhurst Hall. You and Lady Georgiana will be so kind as to make up the rest of the house party, won't you? We'd love to have you. Isn't that right, darling?"

Lyndhurst Hall? House party? Emily's frown mimicked a gathering thundercloud as she tried to digest this latest piece of information. That hadn't been any part of the Plan. What was he talking about? She had no intention of spending time at his brother's estate. Not only that, but one more "darling" and she was going to fling her dish of cherry pudding straight at his head, Emily thought, the idea appealing to her so much she had to force herself to lay down her spoon and clasp her hands together in her lap. "But, *dearest*, surely we can speak of this later? Poor Aunt Hortense has enough to consider at the moment," she said between clenched teeth, her cheeks beginning to ache abominably from the effort of constantly smiling.

"Anything you say, darling," Lord Edward replied, so pleased with himself for having slipped in that bit about the house party, he was oblivious of the fact that his beloved was within Ames Ace of murdering him where he sat.

Once the meal was done, the small party repaired to the main drawing room and Lord Edward surprised everyone by immediately going down on one knee in front of Emily, who had purposely sat in a chair set away from all the others. Pulling a small square box from his pocket, he opened it with a flourish, extracting a golden ring set with a huge yellow diamond. "I'd be honored if you would wear this, Emily. It's been in our family for generations."

Before she could think, before she could come to grips with the fact that this devastatingly handsome, eligible man was kneeling at her feet while her aunt and cousin looked on, she felt her left hand being lifted and the cold metal being pushed onto her finger. She looked down at her hand to see that the diamond, surrounded as it was by at least a dozen smaller stones, spanned her finger from knuckle to knuckle. "It ... it's lovely," she said just as a good *fiancée* ought.

"No, it isn't," Lord Edward told her happily

under his breath. "It's quite the most horrid piece of stone ever unearthed, but it's also the only thing I had in the house that wasn't made for a man. You've been doing splendidly so far, by the way. Nobody suspects a thing. Now, come here—I think I'm supposed to kiss you."

"No, I—" Emily protested feebly, but she was too late. Lord Edward pulled her to her feet and then brushed her lips softly with his own before turning away to accept the duchess's nearly incoherent congratulations, leaving his breathless *fiancée* to stand abandoned in the middle of the room, her mouth at half-mast.

He'd done it again, knocked her into horsetails, while he'd remained completely unaffected. It wasn't fair, that's what it wasn't, and Emily disliked him more at that moment than she ever had. Who did he think he was, trifling with her this way? Kissing her in front of her dotty aunt and romantic cousin just as if he had a right to? How were they ever going to make anyone believe they wished to end an engagement he seemed to be enjoying to the top of his bent?

"Darling?" Lord Edward prompted, squeezing her hand in silent warning. "Your aunt has just offered you her best wishes."

Emily obediently pasted an inane grin back on her face and allowed her relatives to kiss her cheek and gush over the beauty of her ring, all the time looking at Lord Edward out of the corners of her eyes and quietly willing him to remove that smug, satisfied expression from his face.

Just this afternoon he had been ranting and raving enough to bring down the house, proving that he'd rather be visited by the black death than be in the same room with her, and now he was pretending to be deliriously happy to be betrothed. And, poor fools that they were, they *believed* him! If he *did* suddenly take wing and fly thrice around the chandelier, Emily wouldn't even blink!

She was convinced more than ever before that this was all a big game to him, a lark, a delightful rig he was running to amuse himself. He was enjoying himself—he was actually *enjoying* himself! She could hear him now as he explained away this ridiculous engagement, telling everyone how he had wished to set up his nursery and, as he felt sorry for her and thought she'd make a conformable, undemanding wife—the sort a man could leave in the country with his heir and never miss—he had chosen plain Emily Howland to be his convenient, unassuming bride.

People wouldn't laugh at *him*, they wouldn't titter behind *his* back because he'd affianced himself with a woman of no consequence. No, they'd congratulate him for his brilliance, right up to and beyond the point the engagement was called off. Talk about having your cake and eating it too—the man bore off the palm!

Emily's slanted eyes narrowed dangerously as she concluded that, yet again, she was the victim. First the victim of her relatives' ridiculous suppositions, and now Lord Edward's victim as well. He had never really been concerned about her this afternoon when he and his friend Lord Delbert had gleefully pointed out the pitfalls of immediately retracting the duchess's announcement. Oh, no. He had only been thinking of his own reputation, his own ridiculous consequence.

From the moment she had first stepped foot in London she had been acted upon rather than acting, Emily decided, her opinion of her own worth dropping like a stone. She had been a brown wren, allowing people to think her dull and dowdy, allowing them to use her for their own devices.

It was terrible to feel this way, and it wasn't fair—it just wasn't *fair*! Emily's chin began to wobble as her self-pity threatened to overwhelm her. She wasn't a mean person, she wasn't particularly stupid, so she didn't believe she was being punished or only receiving her just deserts. Yet she was a victim.

Lord Edward was leaning toward the duchess, trying to make heads or tails of some story she was telling him about her own wedding trip—if only she could remember if it was Spain or Italy they had visited; it had these lovely little waterways running through it, she knew— and Lady Georgiana was leaning against his arm, the two of them making a heartbreakingly beautiful picture. Emily's heart began to beat hurtfully in her chest, until she could no longer stand there and watch, isolated in the middle of their small group.

Walking over to the window, she stared out into the darkness, seeing her reflection and that of the room behind her in the glass. Slowly, one by one, the tears she had been holding back began to fall. She could drop dead right here and now and none of them would notice, she thought, sniffing, for her nose always ran when she cried. She hated being plain. She . . . absolutely . . . positively . . . hated it!

13

Five days after the dinner party, just as Lord Edward was sitting down to a leisurely luncheon of braised lamb chops, Burton excused himself to answer a loud knocking on the front door. Waving the butler away, Lord Edward served himself, still thinking about his latest attempt to win Emily's heart.

Simmons, her grace's personal maid, had proved most helpful in gaining him a list of Emily's measurements, and after spending the morning in Bond Street he had returned to his town house a happy, if slightly less well-heeled, man. So far, his amended plans had been swimming along quite nicely, and he was finding it increasingly difficult to believe that this confused engagement hadn't been his intention all along.

The first few gowns he had ordered would be ready in less than a sennight, in plenty of time for their removal to Sussex late the next week, and he was already anticipating Emily's sure-to-be-ecstatic reaction to his largess. Not only that, but a discreet peek at Simmons' scribblings had served to put a new spring in his step, for it would seem that his darling Emily was not pudgy, but merely the victim of a sadistic dressmaker. He knew she was going to be beautiful, had known it all along—not that he would have loved her any the less if she had been in need of shedding a few inches.

Now, if he could only find some way of convincing his reluctant darling to have something done with her hair . . .

"There you are, my dearest Noddy! I found you!" came a high, thin voice from the doorway. "Stand up so I may kiss you on both cheeks, for you have made me the happiest of men!"

"Reggie?" Lord Edward threw down his fork and scrambled to his feet, to be immediately clasped in his brother's scented embrace. "I can't believe it. You haven't come into town for years."

"Yes, it is I. Merryvale must be scouring the countryside! Now, stand still, I said, so I might kiss you." Reginald Archibald Sinclair Laurence, fifth Marquess of Lyndhurst, then made good his threat, holding his younger brother slightly away from him by the shoulders before, as promised, planting smacking kisses on both his cheeks. "As I told the dearest Colonel just yesterday—or was it the day before? I'm so bad with dates—Noddy, you are the very best of brothers, an absolute prince of a good fellow! You have saved my life, Noddy, you have set me *free!*"

Lord Edward was confused as well as embar-

rassed. Reggie had always been so demonstra-
tive, so theatrical. His garbled explosions of
delight could be extremely unnerving. Backing
away from him, and trying with all his might
not to raise his hands and scrub at his cheeks,
Lord Edward blustered, "Free, Reggie? I am? I
did? I didn't know . . . er . . . Precisely *what* did
I do, Reggie?"

The fifth Marquess of Lyndhurst lowered his
tall, thin body into the chair Burton held out for
him, affectionately patted the little man on the
top of his bald head before pulling him up onto
his lap like an adored toddler, and then magnanimously motioned for Lord Edward to sit
down as well. "Why, you got yourself engaged
to be wed to the dearest Miss Howland, of course.
Merryvale tried to hide it from me, but I found
it. I always find what he doesn't wish me to
find. It's rather like a game we play. I will like
her, won't I? Oh, I'm sure I will. Noddy, I can't
begin to tell you how wonderful this is. Is that a
new painting, Noddy? I don't think I like it."

Lord Edward looked across the room at the
painting his brother was pointing to, then shook
his head. "No, Reggie, it's not new. You gave it
to me for Christmas three years ago, I think."

"Really? Burton should hide it in the cellars.
It must have been during that time I thought I
adored ducks above all else. But *dead* ducks?
Odd, don't you think?"

"Reggie?" his brother prompted, trying to
bring the conversation back to the reason for
this visit. "How have I saved your life? You

haven't been drinking ink again, have you? You know it makes you sick."

His lordship kissed Burton on both cheeks and then unceremoniously pushed him off his lap. "Ink, Noddy? Don't be silly. I never drink ink anymore; it turns my teeth most dreadfully blue, you know, and it doesn't taste anything as delicious as it looks. But only think—a week ago I was teetering on the brink of despair, just this side of putting a period to my wretched existence—yes, I was, dear boy, I must own it. Oast houses! I ask you, what do I know about oast houses? But now! Well, now I am reborn! A pox on all oast houses, and a pox on Merryvale for denying me my pink cottages! Think about it, Noddy! All the village houses, all in little pink rows. It would be delightful! But, do I care? No! Not I! You see before you a new man, a man with a purpose, a man with a glorious mission in his life. Did I kiss you, Noddy? I want to shower you with kisses!"

Lord Edward shifted uncomfortably in his chair. "Yes, Reggie, you kissed me, and I don't mind telling you that I wish you would try very hard not to do it again." Obviously Reginald was off on another one of his tangents. How had he gotten past Merryvale? "But suicide, Reggie? I thought we had settled that silly business when I visited with you at Lyndhurst Hall. You told me the Reverend Smithers had quite decided you against it."

Lord Lyndhurst nodded vigorously in the affirmative. "Yes, yes, he did, he did, but that was before I met dearest Colonel Musbank and heard of his Great Expedition. Tibet! Living among the monks! The dream of my lifetime at last come to fruition. Can you imagine my joy, my heartbreak, when I thought the good Colonel must leave me behind—that I was sentenced to a lifelong imprisonment at Lyndhurst Hall? They're all yelling for thatch now; as if a little good English drizzle would melt their silly heads!"

"The tenants are asking for new thatch for their cottage roofs?" Lord Edward hazarded, grabbing hold of Burton by the back of his collar as the butler tried to make good his escape from the room.

"Didn't I say that? I wanted them to come live with me, but Merryvale frowned so that I couldn't do it. He's no fun, Merryvale, no fun at all. Well, I cannot begin to tell you of my ravaged emotions to think that the Colonel would depart without me, but then, just at the last moment, just as I was penning you my final correspondence—it was quite a good note, if a tad lengthy, my best yet; I brought it with me so that you may read it at your leisure—the papers arrived from London and I learned that you, dearest boy, had reached out to save me from death's eternal darkness."

Lord Edward looked over at Burton and rolled his eyes at this latest silliness. It wasn't that he discounted Reggie's talk of Tibet and suicide, but he knew well enough that these were just his brother's latest "interests" and he'd never really seriously try to put an end to himself—although he might just try to hike to Tibet with a ham sandwich in his pocket. Two years ago it had been building a balloon large enough to float to America that had occupied his brother's mind, and the year before that it had been the ink episode—with the marquess professing the liquid was good for the spleen. "I did, did I? How wonderful of me, I'm sure. Tell me, Reggie, how did I do this marvelous thing?"

"Why, by becoming engaged to be wed, of course," Lord Lyndhurst told him, unable to believe his brother could not see what was clear as crystal to him. "I've already told you that. Honestly, Noddy, I can't believe you've been attending. I've come to town for the nuptials, and then dearest Colonel Musbank and I are off to Tibet to commune with the monks. Noddy? You're looking most queer. Is everything all right? Don't tell me you're not getting married, for I couldn't bear it, I tell you—I just couldn't *bear* it. Not after the pink cottages. Burton, dearest sprout! Is there a length of strong rope in the house?"

"Going to Tibet, you say? What would anybody want to do that for, for pity's sake? It's not as if there's anything there, is it? I mean ... *Tibet?* It's in Asia somewhere, right? And it's not even part of the Empire, is it? Good God, Ned, what are you going to do? Maybe it's time you gave it up and had dearest old Reggie fitted for his own straight waistcoat."

Lord Edward looked at his friend over the top of his glass, trying hard to focus on Lord Henry Montgomery's drink-blurred features. "He's not mad, Monty. Maybe a little confused, but no more so than your cousin Ferdie. Isn't he the one who thinks he's a tree? Besides, only the poor are mad. The rich are eccentric."

"A rosebush, a pink one, I think," Lord Henry corrected, flushing. "But Ferdie's only a second cousin, and a veritable nobody into the bargain. Your brother's the marquess, for God's sake. Think of the talk! No, there's nothing else for it—you'll have to put him away. Insane asylums are not so terrible—some of the best people are locked up in them."

Lord Edward laughed derisively. "Yes, Monty, I know. Asylums have become quite fashionable. I've heard it said that when you hear that someone has just come 'out,' you don't know if it means they've just been presented or *released*. But not Reginald—I won't even consider it. Our father made me promise him on his deathbed that I'd always watch out for Reggie—and, if needs must, prepare myself for the possibility of having to take his place someday at Lyndhurst Hall. Why else do you think I came to town considering marriage in the first place? My last trip home was a total disaster. Reggie's latest trick is to think up new ways to do himself in. Thank goodness he's so woefully inept at it. It's just a phase, and will pass, like all the others, but for the moment . . ."

Lord Delbert Updegrove, also present in Lord

Edward's private chamber, and also feeling slightly the worse for drink, lifted his massive red head from his chest to ask, "Then what are you going to do, Ned, if you can't bring yourself to disappoint him? Reggie thinks you're going to marry Miss Howland, even though we all know you never meant any such thing until we made such a sad hash of everything. You can't fool us, try as you like. This engagement isn't working. Miss Howland doesn't like you above half, you know, and would make your life a living hell into the bargain, not that I can blame her. But then *you'd* be the one we'd be carting off to Bedlam, and I don't think that's what your father wanted."

Pushing himself to his feet, Lord Edward began pacing up and down the small carpet in the center of the room, glass in hand. Much as he feared telling the whole truth to his friends, he knew the time had come to lay all of his cards on the table. "You're wrong there, Del," he said at last. "I have always meant to marry Miss Howland. I love her."

This bald declaration served to gain Lord Edward his friends' undivided attention and he sat back down to explain all that had transpired to bring them to this point. He told them how he had traveled to Lyndhurst Hall only to find that Reggie was retreating more and more from reality every day, and explained that he had decided then and there that it was time he found a wife and retired to the country to personally take charge of his brother. He told them of seeing

Miss Howland with the dowager duchess, of how levelheaded and understanding she was when confronted with the dowager's vagaries, and how, slowly, he had found himself falling in love with her.

He explained—twice, as Del seemed to have a difficult time taking it all in—why, as Miss Howland paid absolutely no attention to him, he had purposely teased her, trying to make her aware of him, and how he had found it necessary to pay court to Lady Georgiana in order to be with Miss Howland, who refused to step outside the boundaries of a companion and allow herself to be approached as a young lady in her first Season.

He went on to confide his original plan, telling them how he had hoped to invite Lady Georgiana down to Lyndhurst Hall so that he could observe Miss Howland firsthand with his brother. "After all, I could not ask her to take on Reggie with me without first letting her know precisely what she'd be getting herself into, could I?" he pointed out when Lord Henry couldn't seem to understand what Reggie had to do with anything.

Last, he told them how, thanks to their misconception about the relationship between him and that same Miss Howland, he'd had to amend his plan, discovering that being engaged to the woman of his dreams settled the problem of convincing the dowager of the need for a house party. "The only really difficult thing," he admitted, "was making Emily believe I love this engagement as little as she does, or else she never would have agreed to my scheme. I had hoped she would see me in a better light if we could be together as a betrothed couple, and then there would be no need for any more subterfuge. But now Reggie is here and, much as I love him, I do worry that he might just prove to be too much for Emily right now."

"You could be right," Del put in consideringly. "Georgy tells me Miss Howland's been acting most peculiar for an engaged lady, moping about the house and crying into her handkerchief when she thinks no one is looking. Georgy is most upset, the dear girl, though I don't think either she or the duchess suspects the truth. There'd be the devil to pay if they did, I don't mind telling you."

"Crying? I don't like the sound of that," Monty interjected, his poet's soul touched. "Poor girl's been put upon enough as it is, and it's all your fault, Ned. It's a sad thing you love Miss Howland. After all, if you hated her, there's no telling how happy she'd be at this moment. I think you've gone too far this time, and I don't like it one bit, I tell you, that we have helped you to make Miss Howland miserable. You'll have to let her cry off from this engagement and find yourself another, more willing female. And you'll just have to tell Reggie the truth and then hide all the knives—and maybe the drapery sashes."

Lord Edward subsided into his chair once more, wondering why he had bothered to ask his two friends for their assistance. He'd just have to find some way to get Reggie back to Sussex without meeting Emily. Later, after she loved him, he would explain about his eccentric brother.

"Ned?" Monty questioned, interrupting Lord Edward's thought processes. "You're not thinking of putting an end to yourself, are you? I mean, it doesn't run in the family or anything? You never said how your father came to cock up his toes."

"No, Monty," Lord Edward assured him, shaking his head. "I was just thinking how much easier it would be if Emily Howland was like every other female and willing to marry the devil himself for money and a title. I'm even handsome into the bargain. Why, I could name a half-dozen damsels right now who'd marry me in a minute."

"And so modest with it all," Lord Henry inserted, still trying to tell himself that Emily Howland really favored him rather than his friend. She did like his poetry, and she had always listened to him with a great show of interest. Of course, lately she had been rather quiet, almost sullen, but that was to be expected. Being betrothed to Naughty Ned, even if it wasn't a true betrothal, was enough to put any female off her feed. The man was about as constant as a windstorm, much as Lord Henry liked him personally. "A pony says she won't have you."

Lord Delbert frowned. "Betting on it, Monty? Do you really think that's in good taste? I mean, Ned here has asked us for our help."

"May I come in, Noddy? I thought I heard voices. Oh, how nice, you have company. Hello, boys. Do you have red slippers? I do, two pairs, with little deer embroidered on them, but I seem to have left them at home."

The three friends turned in their chairs to see the Marquess of Lyndhurst standing in the doorway in his bare feet, dressing gown, and tasseled nightcap, smiling at them benevolently. The man was a mass of angles, all knees and elbows, even under the heavily quilted banyan, his drooping nightcap sliding down over one eye as he wriggled his long, skinny toes against the carpet. He was so thin, a good puff of wind would have bowled him over. Lord Edward's heart tugged painfully in his chest, for he loved his brother, mildly eccentric or totally insane.

"Come in, Reggie, come in," Lord Edward urged kindly, standing up to introduce his brother to his friends, and then offered him his own seat. "I'm sorry if we woke you. Are you feeling all right?"

"Fine, fine, just fine," the marquess said, nodding so that his nightcap was in danger of slipping entirely off his head. "I wasn't sleeping anyway. I'm too terribly, terribly excited about my trip. Did Noddy tell you that I'm heading off to Tibet, boys? It's all arranged. Is that sherry? I do so favor sherry. Dearest Colonel Musbank and I leave in less than two months, once I'm sure that Noddy here is safely married and settled in at Lyndhurst Hall. My heart is just fluttering and fluttering. I doubt I'll sleep a wink between now and then for sheer excitement. Just think, boys, *Tibet*. How you all must envy me!"

"About as much as I envy a crossing sweep on a rainy day," Del whispered just loud enough for Lord Henry to hear him.

"It's just absolutely delicious, boys," Lord Lyndhurst gushed, oblivious of their total lack of interest. "Dearest Colonel Musbank says we can live like kings for mere pennies—I once gave a penny to a little boy along the road. He was most grateful. He had red hair, like you—emperors, even, not that it matters. It's the land itself that excites me, and the customs. And the monks, the mountains, the beauty—oh, it's just too thrilling! No, I remember now, I gave him my *sandwich*—tongue, I believe—and he was a little girl. How silly of me! Do you think they eat tongue in Tibet? Hah! Tongue in Tibet—it almost rhymes, doesn't it? I cringe, I absolutely *cringe*, I tell you, when I think how close I came to ending it all. It would have advanced me on the wheel of life, the Colonel says, but just think of what I would have missed!"

"Being underground would have put a bit of a crimp in your plans, Reggie, I agree," Lord Edward said kindly, ignoring the subject of tongue sandwiches entirely, "but I wish you wouldn't dwell on such unpleasant thoughts. I've rung for Burton. Why don't you have him fix you something to help you sleep? It has been a long day."

A few minutes later, after Burton had come to lead his lordship away, Monty sighed and said, "He's a sweet-enough crazy man, your brother.

You'll have to marry Miss Howland now, Ned, and have her fall in love with you later. I can't see any other way out of it."

Del rose to his feet, his glass held high. "To Ned and Miss Howland—the best of luck!"

Lord Edward watched as Monty and Del drained their glasses and then flung them into the fireplace. "Thank you, my friends. I have a feeling I'm going to need it."

14

❦

"Miss Howland! Miss Howland, please, you have to wake up straightaway! Oh, *please*, Miss Howland!"

Emily, who had found her rest very late the previous evening only after turning onto her stomach and placing her head beneath her pillow, moaned her protest at this rude awakening before slowly lifting one side of the pillow and peering out with one eye. "Simmons, is that you? It's still dark. Is something wrong? Is it the dowager? I pleaded with her not to eat that fish at Lord Harvey's. It didn't smell quite fresh."

The maid shook her head, then helped Emily to sit up in bed. "No, miss, it's not the old lady, beg your pardon. It's this . . . this *man*. He came knocking on the door fit to wake the dead a little while ago and now he's in the kitchens, eating bread and honey with Cook and all cozy-like. Says he's the Marquess of Lyndhurst, but let me tell you, if that's the marquess, then I'm the Queen of the May. He's a loose screw if ever I saw one. Please, miss, you have to do something!"

Emily squeezed her eyes closed and shook her head to clear it. The Marquess of Lyndhurst? That would be Reginald, Lord Edward's brother. But Lord Lyndhurst was in Sussex, not London. Lord Edward said he never traveled. Besides, when was the last time she'd heard of a marquess taking bread and honey in a strange kitchen at daybreak? Slipping her feet into her slippers, Emily allowed the maid to help her into her dressing gown. "You must be mistaken, Simmons. This sounds like some sort of prank to me. Have you sent for the constable?"

"The constable?" Simmons parroted, aghast. "But, miss, surely we can't! The man may be balmy, but he's Quality, sure as check. We can't have one of the Quality carted off to the guardhouse. Please, miss, let me help you get dressed so you can go see for yourself what we should do before the dowager gets wind of it, or we'll be in it for sure. She'd most likely ask the queer fellow to stay to tea."

Emily sighed. "Oh, very well, Simmons. I'll go. But I'll go as I am, thank you anyway. I'm tired, and I have every intention of returning to bed once this prankster has been routed. Come with me." So saying, Emily tossed her hair— done up in a single long braid for the night but now rather mussed—over her shoulder, gave a sharp tug on the belt of her dressing gown, and headed for the servants' stairs, eager to put an end to such foolishness.

"And so," Emily heard a rather high, thin male voice saying as she stopped in the hallway just outside the open kitchen door, "once I had got all the feathers sewn to my sleeves—plus the three tail feathers, of course, that I had secured to the seat of my unmentionables—I leaned forward as far as possible, then stepped off the edge of the balcony that juts out over the gardens and flapped my arms up and down just as hard as I could."

"Lord love a duck, your worship, you coulda broke yer bloomin' neck doin' a fool thing like that! Wot happened then?" a female voice exclaimed excitedly—obviously the cook, Emily decided as she too waited to hear the rest of the story.

The man laughed, the sound full of wry amusement. "Broke both my ankles, that's what happened, more's the pity. Noddy was very put out about it, but I still say, if the wind had been with me I would have soared into the sky, just like a bird on the wing. But I don't do that sort of thing anymore, you understand, now that Merryvale has come to stay with me. Merryvale frowns on air flight, and prefers that I just keep pigeons. You did say this is where the fair Miss Howland is residing for the Season? As it's Tuesday, I was sure she would be receiving."

Emily stuck her head around the doorway to peek at her early-morning visitor, suddenly apprehensive. The man was well-spoken, even if what he said didn't make much sense, and she was beginning to wonder if there might be some small truth in his assertion that he was the marquess. It wouldn't do to let him see her in her nightclothes, she thought, just as she realized that a marquess who found nothing extraordinary about taking his ease in the kitchens with the servants would probably not even notice her present attire. Besides, Simmons was right. Whoever this odd man was, the dowager would surely be taken with him. He had to be dealt with, and quickly, before the rest of the household roused.

"There she is, yer worship!" Cook crowed, catching sight of Emily, who had lingered too long at the door, struck as she was by the thin man's resemblance to Lord Edward. "Missy, his worship's come ta see ya. Ever so nice, 'e is, too."

"Miss Howland!" the marquess shouted, jumping to his feet and rushing across the bare wooden floor to take Emily's hands in his and pull her more fully into the room. "How good of you to grant me this audience. Please, just stand there and let me look at you. Red slippers! How perfectly delightful! Oh, I knew I would love you. I just knew it!"

"Red is such a pretty color, isn't it? So bright, so cheerful," Emily answered kindly, her heart immediately going out to this strange man. She allowed her hands to remain in his as she stared and stared, no longer caring that she wasn't dressed for company, as it didn't seem to bother her guest in the slightest.

The man looked just like Lord Edward, except for the fact that he was at least a dozen or more years his senior, and he was much, much thin-

ner, his obviously expensive clothing hanging
on his bony frame. His eyes were just the same
shade of light leaf green, although they seemed
to burn with some hidden light that she considered to be almost feverish in nature. He looked
ethereal, fragile, and she suddenly felt protective of him. "Your lordship," she said, smiling
up into his open, innocent face. "How nice of
you to call. Shall we sit down? I believe Cook
has some muffins in the oven, if my nose doesn't
betray me."

With the insight that was often a special gift
of the gentle-minded, Lord Lyndhurst clapped
his hands together happily and proclaimed: "You
like me! Oh, how wonderful. I knew you would,
just as I knew I would like you. Isn't this pleasant? Noddy will be so pleased to know we get
along so well."

"Noddy?" Emily questioned, trying to hold
back her mirth, unable to believe Lord Edward
would ever consent to answer to such a childish
nickname.

His lordship nodded vigorously. "Yes, Noddy.
He's sleeping, you know. Such a slugabed. I
tippy-toed past his door to steal a march on him
with you this morning. After all, we really should
talk about the wedding. Is your father anywhere
about, my dear?"

Emily silently signaled for Simmons to leave
the room and waited until the maid had disappeared before saying, "My father has been dead
for more than six years, my lord, and my mother,
brothers, and sisters reside in Surrey. I am only

in London acting as companion for my cousin, Lady Georgiana, the youngest daughter of the dowager Duchess of Chilworth. But, please, there is no reason to involve yourself. Hasn't your brother explained to you that this engagement is only—"

Once again Emily's hands were captured in his lordship's as the marquess trilled, "Yes, yes, your engagement! Oh, how wonderful it was to read about Noddy's soon-to-be bride. You have saved my life, you know. I had despaired of going to Tibet with the Colonel, but now I can, and with a free heart. Noddy will be taken care of and you may both have Lyndhurst Hall with my blessings! It is just wonderful! You do like the country, don't you?"

Emily's left eyebrow arched ever so slightly as her smile began to show signs of strain around the edges. "Lord Edward hasn't spoken to you about our engagement, has he, your lordship?"

"Please, please, call me Reggie. And I shall call you Dulcinea. I have been reading Cervantes, you see, and it seems such a regal name, fitting for one such as you."

"Well, thank you, my lord. That's very kind of you. Please, tell me more about this Colonel you spoke of a moment ago. You're planning a trip with him—to Tibet, you said? My, that seems so far away, almost another world."

The thin, sensitive face lit up like a fireworks display at this mention of Tibet. "All my life I have searched high and low for an adventure of this magnitude. Truly, all my past adventures are thoroughly cast into the shade with the prospect that now lies before me, ready to be snatched down like a fine ripe apple. Delicious! And now, dear Dulcinea, now that you and Noddy are to be married, I am free to go, free to fly into the face of adventure! I am reborn!"

"Master Reginald! I have run you to ground at last! Shame on you, calling on Miss Howland at this ungodly hour."

"Well, lookee 'ere!" Cook exclaimed, turning to see who had spoken, a wooden spoon coated with hardened bacon grease pointing straight at Burton, who was standing just inside the kitchens. "It's one o' them dwarfs, ain't it? Isn't it cute, all dressed up like it was growed up?"

Burton puffed out his pudgy chest like a rooster about to crow, clearly intending to render Cook a blistering set-down, so that Emily ordered quickly: "Cook, have someone bring us breakfast in the dining room, if you please. Come along, my . . . that is, Reggie. We're only in the way here now that Cook is getting preparations under way for the day's meals."

Burton moved swiftly across the room on his short legs and took hold of the marquess's elbow, having decided that this interview was at an end. "I hesitate to point this out, Miss Howland," he interjected as neutrally as possible, "but you are still dressed in your nightclothes."

Emily looked down at herself and immediately slapped a hand against her mouth. "Oh, my goodness, I completely forgot! We were having such an interesting conversation, you see, and I—"

"Please, Miss Howland, I quite understand, and it's not my place to ask for an explanation," Burton said, accustomed to smoothing over waters either the marquess or Lord Edward had ruffled. "Master Reginald and I shall return to Lord Edward's town house, for Merryvale has come up from Sussex looking for his employer, much agitated, actually, that he should have missed him, and we should strive to calm him as soon as possible. Would it be all right if Lord Edward pays a call in Portman Square later this afternoon? To . . . well, to explain?"

"Merryvale's here? How nice. Now Noddy can tell him it's all right if I go to Tibet. She has red slippers too, Burton," Reggie informed the servant after bowing low over Emily's hand and turning to walk to the tradesmen's entrance he had entered the mansion through earlier. "I have found that only cheerful people wear red, you know. Noddy has done well for himself, don't you think?"

Cook watched them go. "There goes one who's all about in 'is upper works, if ya takes my meanin', miss. But 'e's 'armless, Oi'm thinkin', for all o' that."

"I think he's wonderful!" Emily defended the marquess, her chin held high as she clutched her dressing gown together at the bodice. "Dulcinea," she added more softly. "What a lovely name."

15

"The marquess has arrived in town and is coming here?" The dowager duchess automatically lifted her hands to her head to assure herself that her new wig had not slipped to one side, as it was so distressingly prone to do. "How wonderful! How perfectly . . . um, perfectly . . ."

"Delightful," Emily completed dully, wishing that just once she had a pretty gown to wear.

"Yes, thank you. Delightful," her grace concluded. "Tell me, which marquess would that be, dear?"

"The Marquess of Lyndhurst, Mama," Lady Georgiana supplied as she stood in front of the largest mirror in the drawing room, also inspecting her appearance. "Lord Edward's older brother, Reginald. Del was here this morning and said he's a lovely man. He's come to discuss the wedding, I should imagine. Isn't that right, Emmy?"

Emily perched on the edge of the settee and watched her female relatives flutter about the large room like showy birds reluctant to come to roost. She was alternately looking forward to and dreading the coming interview: looking forward to it because she was human, and hearing the dowager and the marquess converse was bound to be highly entertaining, and dreading it because being obliged to hear them converse about the wedding was most likely going to be extremely uncomfortable. She could find her only solace in the fact that Lord Edward was bound to be as nervous as she concerning the outcome of this afternoon's visit.

How was Lord Edward going to talk his way out of this latest fix? It was one thing to pull the wool over the dowager's eyes—almost too easy to be sporting, actually, if one were to be totally honest—but it was quite another to deliberately mislead the gentle marquess, who seemed to be counting so on this marriage. Oh, why hadn't she refused at the outset to go along with Lord Edward's foolish plan? This pretend engagement was presenting more problems than it was worth.

"Oh, look, Emmy, they're here!" Lady Georgiana exclaimed, peeking out the window that overhung the street. "Oh, my goodness, Lord Edward looks so strange, almost ill. Do you suppose he's sickening for something? Oh, there's the marquess. He's very thin for a marquess, isn't he?"

"Georgy, come away from there at once. You know it's not polite to stare," Emily chided, trying her best not to jump up and join her cousin at the window for some gawking of her own. So Lord Edward was looking ill, was he, poor fellow? Perhaps lying was not as palatable as he had thought it to be, when it involved telling all those shocking rappers only to *her* relatives.

Within a few moments they could hear the rap of the knocker and the three women hastened to seat themselves around the tea tray, doing their best to appear at their ease.

"Good afternoon, ladies," Lord Edward said when the butler had finished announcing them. "May I have the honor of presenting— "

"Oh, dear, that's right," the dowager broke in, her expression of polite greeting crumbling. "Archy's dead. I had forgotten for a moment. Who are you, then?"

The marquess, finding nothing at all unusual in this outburst, went immediately over to the dowager and presented himself, apologizing profusely for not being his father. "But then, alas, I never was, was I, Noddy?"

"That's all right," the dowager responded kindly, adding quietly, "but did you have to be blond? What's your name again?"

"Mama!" Lady Georgiana warned, afraid her mother would go off again on one of her depressing stories about blonds, and Lord Edward quickly completed the introductions, carefully avoiding Emily's sure-to-be-condemning eyes as he did so.

"My sweet Dulcinea!" Reginald exclaimed, bending down to kiss Emily firmly on both cheeks. "I'm in alt. You look even lovelier dressed, my dear. Doesn't she, Noddy?"

Maintaining his emotionless expression with difficulty as he watched the color pour into his beloved's cheeks, Lord Edward quipped, "Not having had the opportunity to observe Miss Howland in *déshabillé*, Reggie, I have nothing with which to compare her appearance. Now, please sit down so that we can have this chat you are so anxious for. We can't stay long, remember? I did tell you that on our way over here."

"Not stay? But there is so much to talk about, isn't there? I mean, with the wedding and all," Lady Georgiana questioned, as Emily had not as yet asked her to be one of her maids, and she was so hoping to be included in the wedding party.

"Miss Howland's mother is in Surrey, Lady Georgiana," Lord Edward interposed reasonably, clearly hoping to postpone any talk of the nuptials until he could speak with Emily alone. "We will of course have to seek her approval before making any definite plans. After all, I have not even officially asked for Miss Howland's hand, have I?"

"Oh, but that's all taken care of," Lady Georgiana said comfortingly, waving away his protest with one hand. "Mama had me send the clipping to Aunt Minerva in Surrey straightaway, with a letter explaining everything. Mama said it was only proper, Emily, so stop frowning at me. Somebody has the measles, and your mama expects the rest to come down with them, so she warned us to keep you away, as it's not good for someone in your condition to be around illness. Didn't I tell you, Emmy? Aunt Minerva says all's not just as she hoped it would be, but Lord Edward seems to be a good man who is doing as he ought at last. And she forgave Mama completely, so everything is just fine."

"You . . . you told my mother?" Emily asked, her voice strangled as she looked to Lord Edward for help. "Why didn't anyone tell me about this? Just what did you and Aunt Hortense tell my mother, Georgy? Surely you didn't tell her that I was—"

"To be married in August!" Lord Edward fairly shouted, drowning out Emily's next words. "That's what they wrote, I'm sure. Isn't that right, Lady Georgiana?"

Lady Georgiana nodded firmly, then added, "That, and that Emily's increasing, of course. Oh, my goodness! Mama! We never wrote back, did we? Isn't that strange, that we forgot something so important."

Immediately panicking, Lord Edward quickly looked over to his brother, who had been sitting beside Emily, munching on a macaroon, hoping the marquess's mind was off on one of its tangents and he hadn't been attending—but it was not to be.

"Increasing? Dulcinea's going to have a *baby*?" Reginald's bright green eyes were immediately filled with tears and he turned to Emily, his delighted smile lighting the entire room. "A baby," he said, sighing and clasping his hands to his chest, accepting the news without any hint of censure. "Dulcinea, you have made me the happiest of men!"

The dowager was confused. "But I thought the other blond was the father, Emily. Why is the marquess so happy? I don't understand."

It is an acknowledged fact that, regardless of gender, education, or natural intelligence, persons of quality cannot be expected to function in this world with any reasonable level of competence without the support and guidance of the people belowstairs—their loyal servants.

They might wage war successfully without them, they might even annex colonies, invest their money wisely, and recklessly gamble away fortunes without them, but when it came to finding direction in their personal lives, the rudder that guided them—the firm hand that steered them in the correct direction, away from treacherous reefs and dangerous currents—was nearly always to be discovered taking his or her daily mutton in the servants' dining room.

And so it was for Emily and Lord Edward as Burton and Simmons, two champions of the high art of leading their masters around by their aristocratic noses, decided it was high time to take matters into their own capable hands. *Something*, they knew, had to be done to end this foolishness and bring Miss Howland and his lordship together once and for all, and it was clearly up to them to do it.

If it hadn't been clear from the outset that extraordinary measures were called for, the reasonableness of their arguments for interfering had been brought home to them with a vengeance by the events of that afternoon, for, by all accounts, there had been a rare to-do in her grace's drawing room that had ended with the marquess declaring that the wedding would take place within a week, and Miss Howland racing from the room vowing that she'd rather die in a gutter than marry an unfeeling monster like Lord Edward, who had dared to yell at a man as sweet as the marquess!

"Besides," Simmons had declared as Burton handed her the box containing the first of the gowns Lord Edward had ordered—thinking to surprise Emily with her new wardrobe once they were at the house party at Lyndhurst Hall—"she's rather a sweet child, Burton, and not at all stuffy. I like her. I really do like her."

"Are you sure you can get Miss Howland to agree to wear the gown? After all, it is a gift from Lord Edward. He loves her, you know, Simmons, even if she does detest him, now more than ever, and he says he won't force her to marry him, no matter how much he wants it."

"Don't you go fretting about a thing," Simmons had assured him. "I promise you, she's head over ears in love with your young master, though I'm sure I don't know why, for never have I seen such a sorry mix-up. Miss Howland will listen to reason. Besides, I've acted as her personal maid a time or two; *I've* seen her in her tub. I tell you, Burton, you let me have the dressing of her and we'll have his lordship on his knees at her feet in a trice, explaining everything."

Burton reached up his hand to wave a pudgy finger in the maid's face. "There is no need to descend to such plain talk, Simmons," he had pointed out, happy to remind her of just who was in charge of this enterprise. "I'll not have our Miss Howland made over into a common streetwalker."

"And neither will I!" Simmons had protested hotly. "Just like every other man, aren't you, Burton? You drool and ogle with the best of them, I'll wager, but just let a female talk about such things and you go all stuffy and condemning. Well, let me tell you, a wife has just as much right to display her wares as a Covent Garden opera dancer—maybe even more. After all, they're wives, and considered part of the household, just like that silver I was working on earlier when you came visiting to tell me of your plan. If we servants keep the silver shining and sparkling, why shouldn't we be putting a dab or two of polish on a fine miss like Miss Howland? Now, be back here tonight and I'll hold you up and let you peek through the door with me when Miss Howland comes downstairs."

After spending several hours lying in bed in her darkened room, Emily found that her headache, if not her extreme embarrassment, had at last disappeared, and she called out "Enter" when she heard someone scratching on her door. "Simmons?" she questioned, seeing that her aunt's maid was carrying a large package.

"This just arrived, miss. You'll have to hurry if you want to have Mr. Roberto do your hair for the party tonight."

Emily blinked twice in the near-darkness, trying to clear her head. "Mr. Roberto? Isn't he Lady Georgiana's new hairdresser? Why would I want him to do my hair? And I'm not going to Lady Rathburn's party—I've already told everybody that. After this afternoon's debacle, I'm surprised anybody could think that I would."

Simmons nodded sympathetically, understanding Emily's feelings, but pushed on: "But this is a gift from his lordship. Burton delivered this himself, having picked it up personally this afternoon. You wouldn't want to hurt his lordship's feelings, would you, him being such a nice man and all?"

"His lordship?" Emily questioned blankly. "Oh, you must mean the marquess. Isn't that nice. Well, in that case I guess I might at least try the thing on."

Prudently keeping her lips sealed, Simmons only laid down the box and led Emily over to her dressing table. "You just sit here and I'll ring for some tea and a light snack. You'll just have to miss dinner tonight, miss. Then Mr. Roberto can do your hair for you."

"But, Simmons," Emily asked, "can't I first see the gown the marquess sent me?"

"Oh, that must be Mr. Roberto knocking on

the door now!" Simmons sang out gratefully, ignoring Emily's question.

An hour later Emily's bedroom floor was littered with snippets of reddish-brown hair and Mr. Roberto had finished abusing her head with the hot curling stick.

"We now take this like so on either side, and then wrap it—ever so softly, ever so smoothly—draping it along the side of the cheekbone on either side before lifting it, lifting it—so!— and securing it all with miss's best pins. Are you watching? This is important, so very important. The curls are always to be large, soft, cascading down the back like a magnificent waterfall—*so!*—with nothing, *nothing*, but smoothness about the face. It gives to the head a softness, you see, to bring out the miss's fine eyes, to lift the lips, the cheekbones, to frame the face—not to bury it."

The hairdresser stood behind Emily for a moment, admiring his creation, before pulling out the pins and running his fingers through her hair, destroying the effect. Then, standing back slightly, he bowed, indicating that Simmons was to take his place. "Practice, practice, practice. It is the key. I have cut the hair with magic in my scissors. There is much now that can be done with the hair, with my genius to guide you, to show you the way. We can make the curls caress the neck, or have the entire head severe, dramatic, full, but with no curl at all. The possibilities are endless with such hair, with such a head. No, no, *no!*" he scolded, pushing Simmons away. "Not like that—like *this!*"

The "head," strangely, wasn't in the least offended at being treated as if she were an inanimate object. She was sitting in front of her dressing table, staring wide-eyed at her reflection in the glass, an inane smile on her face.

Within the next hour Simmons succeeded in dragging Emily away from the mirror long enough to submerge her body in the tub and then climb into her undergarments. But, with victory in sight, and the new gown in place, her mistress finally balked.

"I can't do it. I won't do it! It ... it's *obscene!* That's what it is, **Simmons,** it's obscene." It's also rather chilly, Emily decided, raising her hands to cover the wide expanse of neckline visible above the startling *décolletage* of the thin, ivory-colored silk gown.

"You look fine as ninepence," Simmons argued, personally removing Emily's protective hands and placing them at her sides. "You promised to trust me, miss, if you'll remember. Wasn't I right about your hair? And that small bit of rouge and lip paint you finally let me use? And it's impossible to change into another gown— you're going to be late as it is. The dowager and Lady Georgiana went along without you an hour ago, and his lordship is downstairs, cooling his heels and waiting for you to join him. Now, please, Miss Emily, you don't want to disappoint his lordship, do you? You look beautiful."

Emily turned this way and that, inspecting herself in the mirror. The marquess might be the teeniest bit vague, but he certainly had wonderful taste. "I do look rather nice, don't I, Simmons? But . . . but the gown is cut so *low,* and Mama always said—"

"If I may be so bold, Miss Emily, your *mama* is in Surrey," Simmons pointed out rationally, knowing she was just one short step from exasperation, "and *you* are here." She and Burton had been planning for this night an entire week, and she didn't need for her mistress's case of cold feet to ruin everything now. "You don't really want to wear one of your old gowns, do you, with your hair looking so pretty and all?"

Lifting a hand to her throat and the deep rose silk ribbon the maid had secured there, Emily looked at herself one more time, a small, satisfied smile playing about her lips. "All right, Simmons, you win. But if everybody laughs at me at Lady Rathburn's—and if Lord Edward dares to say so much as one nasty word—I vow I'll never, *never* forgive you!"

16

The clock in the hall struck the hour of ten, rousing Lord Edward from his disquieting thoughts to wonder yet again what was keeping Emily. Did she think to merely frighten him with her tardiness, or had she decided to keep him cooling his heels until he gave up and went away without her? They had to talk, dammit; they had to discuss what they were to do next, how they were to coax Reggie back to Lyndhurst Hall without hurting him—and without Emily making things stickier by repeating that she didn't want to marry him. Surely she could see that!

Walking over to a side table, he poured himself another fortifying drink, remembering the look on Emily's face that afternoon as she had ordered him to *do something* and then taken her leave from the drawing room, and rethinking the saying that had something to do with confession being good for the soul. After all, once back in his town house, with Reggie tucked up for his nap and Merryvale standing guard outside his bedroom door, Lord Edward had been forced to endure Burton's lengthy homily on the worth of telling the truth, until he had been happy to return to Portman Square to have everything out once and for all with Emily. Then, if she didn't kill him, they could begin once more at the beginning, with all of his cards finally on the table, and he could court Emily the way she deserved.

Which he could only do if she'd come downstairs before his second thoughts had him scurrying for the door, his tail between his legs. Where the devil was she? Reginald had gone off to Lady Rathburn's with the dowager and Lady Georgiana hours ago, as had those two troublemakers Monty and Del, who seemed to be quite taken with Lord Lyndhurst. What a rare treat society was in for tonight, with the dowager calling Reggie "Archy" while flirting with him outrageously, and Reggie telling anyone who would listen all about his plans for his as-yet-unborn nephew or niece.

This final thought had the power to send him seeking refuge once more in drink, and as he realized his glass was empty, he walked back to the side table and spilled a generous amount into the glass.

"Lord Lyndhurst? Please forgive me for having kept you waiting so long."

Lord Edward froze where he stood, his glass halfway to his lips, his back to the drawing-room door. "Emily?" he asked weakly, suddenly wanting nothing more than to bolt from the room, and wondering if he would have been a white feather had he served under Wellington, taking to his heels the first time he laid eyes on a charging Frenchman. But no, he would be no coward when it came to facing death, he was sure. But facing these next few minutes with Emily—that was another question entirely.

Slowly, still holding on to the glass as if it would protect him in the event of attack, Edward turned to face his accidental *fiancée*.

"Oh, it's you," Emily breathed, suddenly self-conscious. "I . . . I had thought the marquess was waiting for me."

It was quiet in the room for quite some time, as Burton and Simmons, who were hiding in the hall just outside the door, their ears pressed hard to the panels, could attest, before Lord Edward at last rediscovered his voice. *"Emily?"* they could hear him question disbelievingly, his voice a hoarse whisper. "My God, Emily! I had thought, hoped . . . but, I can't believe . . . Well! Can that be you?"

Although Simmons and Burton were righteously beside themselves with glee upon hearing these astonished accents—spending the next few moments silently clapping each other on the back in a mutual display of congratulation—they would have laughed out loud if they could see his lordship's reaction to the altered appearance of the love of his life.

He was, in a word, dumbfounded. He was also

many other things: confused, delighted, awestruck, even somewhat light-headed.

Mostly, his lordship was thankful. Yes, Lord Edward was profoundly *thankful*. She was wearing one of the gowns he had purchased for her. Surely this meant she had forgiven him for the debacle of that afternoon.

She was lovely. No! "Lovely" was too tame a word. She was beautiful! Gorgeous! Breathtaking! He blinked twice and swallowed down hard on the lump in his throat. Where did he start? What did he look at, consider, marvel over, first?

Her hair—that glorious crown that caressed her perfectly formed head, those soft, warm red-brown curls that clung to her slim throat?

Her eyes—those exotic, slanted, deep brown, heavy-lidded eyes that sparkled and bewitched and beguiled?

Or those strong, high cheekbones ... that strangely arrogant nose ... that smooth, flawless skin ... that wide, generous, moist pink mouth?

Then there was her body! Oh, God, yes, his lordship groaned silently, her body. Like an ungainly caterpillar that has somehow shed its shapeless cocoon and taken to the skies as an exotic butterfly, Emily's body had sloughed off the heavy, high-necked monstrosities he remembered and clothed itself in glory.

The gown itself was a marvel that defied explanation, an inspired design fashioned of soft, almost transparent ivory silk. It appeared to begin just under the center of her breasts, then fan out in every direction to drape in folds that barely captured each of her breasts into separate silken cages and molded her hips as they flowered beneath the tiniest waist he'd ever seen. As she took two small hesitant steps into the room, the material clung lovingly to her legs, giving him a clear mental picture of what they would look like without that thin covering.

His gaze returned to her breasts, almost reluctantly, for no matter what wonderful part of her he concentrated on, it could only be because he was not concentrating on another, equally appealing part of her.

He didn't understand. Where could those magnificent breasts have been hiding, even beneath the ugly gowns she had chosen to wear? It was sinful, that's what it was, he thought angrily, to cover up such lush beauty. His palms itched expectantly as he almost succumbed to the need to touch them, to softly sculpture their exquisite shape with his palms, to trace their perfection with his tingling fingertips.

Had he died? Was this heaven? Was any of this really happening? How had he, a poor mortal, gotten so lucky? There was a problem? What problem? Reggie? Reggie who?

"Lord Edward? Are you all right? You look so strange." Emily was having trouble understanding the shocked expression on his face. But, no, this was more than shock, though, thankfully, certainly less than amusement. He was completely nonplussed. Slowly, and perhaps meanly, although she *had* been sorely tried by the man in the past, Emily realized that she rather liked him this way—off his stride, caught off guard, and totally at a loss for speech. It was a decidedly delicious feeling, being in charge of a situation, being the one person who knew what was going on, and she felt the corners of her mouth lifting in a satisfied smile.

"Good Lord, Emily, I can't believe it! What's happened to you?"

So, she thought happily, he's found his voice at last. "Whatever do you mean, my lord?" she questioned carefully, taking a few more steps into the room. She had noted his expression when he had seen the way the ivory silk moved along with her body when she had walked, and saw no reason to deny him another look. She was more than happy; she was **fast** becoming drunk with delight. "I've had my **hair** cut—and your brother was kind enough to make me a gift of this gown. Are you disappointed in the result?"

"Disappointed?" The single word came out as a choked croak, and Emily had to look away quickly for fear she would break into delighted giggles. "A man would have to be out of his mind—that is, no, *no*, I'm not disappointed. A change of . . . a different way with your hair, you say . . . and a new gown . . . is that all?"

Emily sat down, carefully arranging her demi-train as she lowered herself onto the settee, then sat erectly, her shoulders back, knowing she was giving him an unimpeded view of her daring *décolletage*. She felt giddy, dizzy with her power to disconcert this man. "You wouldn't wish to know all my secrets, would you, Edward?" she teased, daring to call him by name, and then blushing as she realized that her words, meant to refer to Simmons' deft hand with the rouge pot, could be interpreted in more than one way.

Afraid that his answer to her artlessly asked question was already in his eyes, that his reaction had been too revealing, too obvious, Lord Edward took refuge in the contents of his glass, swallowing the wine in one long gulp before realizing that he was drinking far too much too early in the evening. Especially this particular evening, one during which his main objective should be remaining in complete control of himself.

"Emily," he inquired solicitously, manfully removing his gaze from her neckline and trying not to sob out loud over his loss, "would you care for a small glass of sherry? We need to talk before joining the others at Lady Rathburn's. As it is, heaven only knows what rumors our dear friends are circulating about us now."

Although they were unchaperoned and really should be leaving, the idea of a single sherry did seem appealing, and Emily accepted his offer, careful not to spill any of the liquid on her new gown. As she sat and sipped, and Lord Edward stood and gawked—there was really no other word for it, she knew with a thrilling flutter of her pulse—Emily at last realized that the only conversation taking place in the room was her internal dialogue with herself, and she was suddenly nervous all over again.

"I imagine when you say we should talk that you are referring to the incident of this afternoon?" she asked, looking up at him through her eyelashes as she had seen debutantes do to such effect while she had sat on the sidelines, blending with the woodwork.

"I did—that is, *I do, I do*." Oh, this is good, Lord Edward thought, mentally kicking himself. Suddenly he possessed all the eloquence of the village idiot. "To be precise, we need to discuss my brother."

Emily's features softened at the thought of the marquess. "I like your brother very much, Edward," she replied earnestly, once again using Lord Edward's name without his title. "He's sweet. I mean, look at this gown. He must have scoured London to find anything this beautiful on such short notice."

Lord Edward lowered his eyelids and shifted his eyes from right to left assessingly, realizing that he was actually jealous of his brother, but wondering if it would be worth his while to contradict Emily, for, after all, if he admitted to ordering the gown—to ordering a half-dozen gowns, actually—she would probably run straight back upstairs and hop into one of her depressing brown shrouds. Could he chance such a tragedy? No! "Yes!" he concurred, his decision made in favor of the new Emily. "Reggie is a prince of a fellow. Now, if we could only discuss how we're going to get that prince of a fellow safely back down to Sussex with his keeper, I'd be greatly gratified."

"His *keeper?*" Emily exclaimed in sudden anger. "What a horrid thing to say! You should be ashamed of yourself. Heaven knows *I'm* ashamed to be hearing such nonsense. Oh, don't think I didn't notice how you kept trying to shush Lord Lyndhurst this afternoon. Why, if that lovely man is in need of a keeper, then half the *ton* should be locked up."

Hearing this indignant outburst, Lord Edward sat down, dropped his chin into his hand, and grinned in delight. He had known she would like Reggie, sweet darling thing that she was, but he had had no idea he'd find himself in the position of defending himself against her affection for the eccentric nobleman. "Emily," he began carefully, "please forgive me for calling Merryvale a keeper—it was an unfortunate description, I agree. Believe me when I say that I love my brother very much. But you must admit that Reggie shouldn't be running tame through society. I mean, it would open him up to such ridicule. I'd hate to see him hurt."

"Or see yourself embarrassed by his rather outgoing manner," Emily added unhelpfully. "But I don't see what all the fuss is about. After all, his lordship told me just this morning that he's leaving shortly on an expedition to Tibet."

"You'd countenance such an expedition?" Lord Edward asked in sudden consternation. "Are you out of your mind? Reggie's never been able to cross the street alone without getting into some sort of scrape."

"He made it to London on his own, even if he

did forget his slippers, which isn't the least surprising, for I'm sure he's never had to pack for himself before," Emily pointed out rationally, her chin tilted in defiance as she defended his lordship. "And if he's not exactly sharp as a tack, he's certainly at least as lucid as the dowager, and nobody's locked her away in the country."

"It isn't from lack of trying, I've heard," Lord Edward grumbled. "Why do you think you were sent along when the duchess insisted upon presenting Lady Georgiana? I doubt your mother, though I'm sure she's a wonderful person, has been totally honest with you, my dear."

Emily frowned, as Lord Edward's dart had hit home. Her mother had spent an unconscionable amount of time instructing her daughter on the care and feeding of the dowager before the stagecoach had carried Emily from Surrey. Not liking where her thoughts were taking her, Emily shot back defensively: "That has nothing to do with the matter at hand. We are discussing your brother."

"I want him home, in Sussex," Lord Edward declared, his handsome face suddenly looking almost mulish. "He's canceled his expedition to Tibet, by the way—not that I ever had any intention of allowing him to go there, any more than I allowed him to sail alone to America in a fifteen-foot sloop, which was his last brainstorm —having decided that it will be much more exciting to stay here in England, awaiting the birth of 'dearest Dulcinea's child.'"

"Oh, no!" Emily's tender heart was touched by this news. "He was so delighted this afternoon, wasn't he? I had hoped you were able to explain the mix-up once you had returned to your town house."

"Do you perchance mean 'explain' in the same way *you* have been so far unable to 'explain' the mix-up to your aunt and cousin?" Lord Edward chided, to prove his point. "As happy as I am that Reggie has given up this Tibet business so easily, I can't say that I'm thrilled to think that we're sitting here arguing while Reggie and the dowager are at Lady Rathburn's telling everyone about our forced 'nuptials' next week."

Emily could feel tears prickling behind her eyes as her hurt and frustration bubbled to the surface. How he hated having his name linked with hers. Did he have to make his dislike so obvious? After all, it was his teasing that had led to her problem in the first place. "Well, what do you propose we do about it," she challenged, "seeing that pretending this engagement was real was all your idea?"

Hearing the sob in her voice, Lord Edward hurried across the room and dropped to his knees at Emily's feet, still the anxious male, still rushing his fences, still hoping deep in his heart to have everything he wanted given to him without first owning up to his machinations, without first paying his dues for seeking to play romantic games with the one woman in the world he truly loved. Pulling his handkerchief from his pocket, he blotted a tear from her cheek, saying, "Please don't cry, Emily. I'm probably just overreacting, not having expected Reggie to show up here, but only for you to meet him at Lyndhurst Hall, and you do like him, just as I hoped you would, so it isn't all that bad, is it? I promise you, my beautiful darling, I'll find a way to put everything right, honestly. I never meant to hurt you."

It was a nice speech, if rather garbled, and Emily didn't believe it for a minute. Lord Edward had never gone out of his way to be nice to her before. On the contrary, she had often thought that he stayed awake nights trying to devise new ways to insult her, like that time he'd had the nerve to pretend to propose to her. Still, she allowed him to dab tenderly at her tears, her chin held high, her eyes deliberately avoiding his as her gaze darted around the room.

His lordship was many things, but he was not stupid. He knew Emily didn't believe him. *He* didn't believe him! To Emily's way of thinking, he had spent the past month in a one-man campaign bent on sending her screaming back home to Surrey, never to show her head in London again, only to end up betrothed to her. Their courtship had been a sham and their engagement was a travesty. Why on earth should she believe he had meant any of it? "Emily, my dear girl—" he began, not really knowing what to say, where to begin.

"No!" she protested, cutting him off. Did he think she had just come down in the last rainfall? She wasn't about to be taken in by this new, seemingly caring Lord Edward. It was this sudden change, this transformation Simmons and Mr. Roberto had worked on her that had him belatedly acting the gentleman with her. He had come to Portman Square tonight to ask for her help—again—only to find that his *fiancée* had been turned into a passably attractive person. "My beautiful darling" indeed! He probably found it more difficult to be insulting to well-dressed females than to unattractive companions.

"Emily? You must believe I'm sorry for everything," he pressed on, still kneeling at her feet. "I know I've hurt you, my dearest. As a matter of fact, I've spent these last weeks since meeting you examining my conscience."

Emily looked down at him and slowly raised one winglike eyebrow. "Only three weeks, Edward? I doubt you allowed yourself enough time to even scratch the surface. But forgive me—I interrupt. Please do continue. What did this examination reveal?"

Oh, she was angry, Edward thought, wincing. She was trying to hide it, but she was very, very angry, and her bewitching smile was definitely gone. Perhaps employing the handkerchief so intimately was pushing his show of concern too far. Perhaps he should change the subject, and concentrate again on their plans concerning Reggie.

Then, just as he was about to say something comforting to the effect that Reggie would soon forget this business about a baby, Emily stuck out the tip of her pink tongue to capture a tear-drop that had slipped into the corner of her mouth, and Lord Edward was lost. "Good Lord, Emily," he said, his hands clenched around his handkerchief for fear he'd otherwise launch himself at her, "don't you know? I love you!"

"Wh-what?" Emily's fingers gripped the arms of her chair as Lord Edward, caught up in the emotion of the moment, rose to his full height in front of her. She felt his hands grasp her shoulders and she allowed herself to be brought to her feet, facing him, her eyes wide, her pulse pounding in her ears.

He looked so sincere, so passionately intense, and he was so terribly, terribly close to her. She could see the sparkles in his eyes as he looked down on her, watch his lips move as he said something to her that the loud rushing in her ears kept her from understanding. His hands were warm, caressing, as they ran along her collarbones, his body hard yet inviting as he drew her so very slowly against it.

She allowed her head to slip to one side as Edward nuzzled at the base of her throat, her eyes closing while she stole this one moment of happiness, this one perfect time that was surely not too much to ask for, considering what she knew she must do.

Now, her little voice screamed, now is the time to push him away, to tell him that he's mistaken, that he is just reacting to a little paint and silk, that the Emily Howland he has always disdained is still locked inside these new, pretty wrappings.

Just a moment more, just one single, sweet moment more, she told the little voice as Edward's lips blazed a trail across her cheek and claimed her mouth.

And in that moment—that one single, sweet moment she had begged her intelligent self to grant her—Emily forgot to resist. All her sane reasoning, all her devastatingly humbling deductions were tossed to the winds as her arms slid up Lord Edward's muscular chest and her fingers twined together in the heavy blond curls at the nape of his neck. Her mind shut down completely as her body, that body she had hidden for years, denying its needs, asserted itself.

Her breasts tingled pleasurably as they made firmer contact with Lord Edward's chest and her legs turned to jelly as she felt the pressure of his knee as it slid between hers. Clinging to him, allowing him to support her weight, Emily opened her lips on a sigh and allowed him entry. She was all fluid, all sensation. She was his, and he was hers. Hers for the taking, hers for the giving, hers for the moment, and let the devil take the hindmost. Tomorrow she would think about the rights of it, the wrongs of it. But tonight would be hers . . .

"Oh, Emily, you're so beautiful, so very beautiful. I love you. Tell me that you love me," Lord Edward whispered breathlessly against her ear, and the spell was broken. Emily stepped back a single pace, her eyes wide as she stared up at

Lord Edward. She could feel her breathing deepen as her heart thumped hurtfully in her breast. All she had to do was smile, acknowledge his statement with just a small nod of her head, and he would sweep her into his arms again. A small voice deep inside her brain urged her to take what he was offering, to take it with both hands, for this was what she had always wanted, from the first moment she had seen his handsome face, from the first moment his lips had claimed hers in that kiss on her aunt's balcony. This was what she had dreamed about, this was what she had secretly hoped for as she gave herself over to Simmons' capable hands. These were the words she had believed could make her happy, could make her whole.

Well, she thought incredulously as she abruptly pushed herself out of his arms, I'll say one thing for you, Emily Howland—when you're wrong, you aren't wrong by half-measures, you're really, *really* wrong!

"Emily, you come back here this . . . er . . . Darling! Where are you going? Didn't you hear me? I said I love you." Lord Edward was confused as he stared after her departing form. "Emily?" he repeated, collapsing into her empty chair in chagrin as he realized she wasn't coming back. "Women! There's no pleasing them. *Now* what did I do wrong?"

Simmons and Burton, who had nearly been discovered peeking in the doorway as Emily bolted so swiftly from the room, and who had hastily retired below stairs to share a pot of tea and commiserate with each other, could have told his lordship precisely what he had done wrong—and, in Burton's case, could have done it through the use of some very colorful language. This opportunity not presenting itself, it was up to Lord Edward to find his way home alone—his worries about the harm the dowager and his brother could cause forgotten—to consume a decanter of port, and, sigh, hatch yet another plan . . .

17

The remainder of the gowns Lord Edward had ordered arrived the next morning in Portman Square, bearing a card upon which the following was scribbled in a sloping, thoroughly masculine hand: "Forgive a besotted fool for trying to gild the lily. With all my Love, Ned."

The card, ripped into precisely twelve pieces, was ceremoniously deposited into Emily's empty teacup.

The gowns, save the lovely sprigged-muslin one Simmons lowered over her head before Emily joined Lady Georgiana and the dowager duchess for breakfast, and the elegant creation she planned to wear that evening to dinner, were lovingly put away in the cupboard in her room.

Emily was angry, yes, but she wasn't so foolish as to snip off her nose merely to spite her face!

She had then gone on to enjoy her day, having spent most of the morning outside in the small garden getting to know the marquess better before that sweet man departed for Sussex with Merryvale (a jolly retired schoolmaster who seemed to sincerely like the marquess), promising to order the refurbishing of the Lyndhurst nursery "as soon as may be" once he was home— employing "dozens of cute little bunnies, you know, with those soft, puffy tails, and they're good luck too, I believe," as the central theme for the wallpaper and other decorations if possible.

This piece of news also cheered Emily, no matter what her thoughts on "cute little bunnies," as she felt it only served to prove that Lord Edward was having the same amount of success explaining away her supposed pregnancy to his brother as she herself had been experiencing with the dowager.

Her afternoon was then whiled away pleasurably enough in keeping an eye on Lady Georgiana and the recently attentive Lord Delbert during a stroll in Green Park as she pretended not to notice the many admiring glances that were being thrown her own way.

It was only after dinner that Emily's mood reverted to melancholia, for the dowager announced that Lord Edward had earlier sent round a note particularly requesting Emily's presence in his box at the theater that evening. The mere mention of his lordship's name brought a flush of embarrassed color flooding into her cheeks, while her spine stiffened as she remembered the way the man had positively drooled over her just because of a slight alteration in her appearance.

Not only that, she reminded herself, but he had then proceeded to make an utter fool of her, spouting that nonsense about loving her and then taking advantage of her weakened condition to kiss her witless. Oh, no, Emily wasn't about to be his guest at the theater that night—not unless pigs suddenly sprouted wings!

Immediately pleading a headache—so that the dowager was pushed to comment that the child, who had been looking rather decent that day, seemed to be prone to sickness, and why Minerva had ever foisted such a fade-away miss on her, she'd never know, except that she was sure Minerva never liked her above half—Emily retired to her bedchamber, donned her oldest nightgown, and climbed into bed, determined not to cry herself to sleep again.

Emily awakened slowly just after midnight, lit the candle at her bedside, then stretched out to her full length on the soft bed, feeling pleasantly warm and curiously contented. She had been dreaming about her meeting with Lord Edward the previous evening, and had fortunately wakened while the dream was still in its early, pleasant stages, just after her entrance into the drawing room—armed with a bit of paint, a cunning hairstyle, and a scandalously gorgeous gown of ivory silk.

And, she remembered, crossing her arms behind her head and grinning up at the ceiling, she *had* been a fabulous success—at least she had for a while. Her smile slowly faded as she remembered how the magical evening had skidded to an abrupt halt once Lord Edward had made his ridiculous declaration and taken her in his arms.

What a revelation that had been! Emily had thought her newfound beauty to be the answer to all her problems, her entry into the happy world of the physically attractive, where one danced all through the night and the world was always wonderful. Lord Edward's reaction to her changed appearance had rudely brought her awake to some of the least-looked-for results of physical beauty.

As he had taken her in his arms, Lord Edward couldn't have cared less if she'd had a brain like a leaky bucket—like that adorable widgeon cousin of hers, Lady Georgiana. Oh, no. Lord Edward had fallen in love—or at least had told Emily he had been *thinking* about falling in love—with Georgy's shell, her outside, her neatly displayed veneer. And now he was doing it again, only this time it was *her* newly attractive shell that was calling to his silly masculine emotions.

Emily's worst enemy all her life, her mirror, had always told her that she was plain. Now that same mirror was telling her that she had somehow become almost beautiful—and that mocking piece of glass was *still* her worst enemy!

The last of her happiness disappeared as a frown wrinkled her smooth forehead. And what absolutely *miserable* timing she had, to pick last night of all nights to allow Simmons to work her magic! If only Lord Edward had encountered her alone and unchaperoned in the drawing room that night, looking just as plainly dowdy as usual, and immediately taken her into his arms and declared his love for her, Emily could have believed him.

The thought brought her up short and she gave a short, rueful laugh. Believed him? How could she delude herself that way? She would have had someone immediately fetch the closest physician, feeling sure Lord Edward had come down with a delirium-inducing fever!

But, be that as it may, Emily decided she had to consider his reaction and how it was related to her altered appearance. Now that he had made it so very clear that her new good looks were attractive to him, she would never know if he wanted her for herself or for her pleasing exterior—or, she reminded herself, that he really wanted her at all.

She already knew, she admitted on a small sigh as she threw back the bedcovers and stood up in the darkened room. After all, he hadn't been staring bug-eyed at her "mind," had he? He "loved" her because Simmons had painted her lips and cheeks with rouge, outlined her eyes with kohl, and then sent her downstairs in half a gown, like some Covent Garden strumpet showing off her wares!

Poor dear Edward, she thought guiltily, and without realizing she was being most horridly immodest, she really shouldn't be too angry with

him. He had really never known what hit him;
he had never stood a chance against the new,
improved Emily. He had been dazzled past the
point of rational thought. After all, he was a
man, wasn't he, and therefore easily dazzled?

As she walked over to the cupboard that held
her new gowns, she knew she would have to
explain his error to him—the poor darling. It
wouldn't be fair to let him continue thinking he
could be in love with her. But for now, for just a
little while, would it be that awful if she closed
her eyes to the truth and wallowed in his affection, like a pig in a trough? She could also
search for a better analogy while she was at it,
but she'd had hardly any sleep in two days and
she refused to dwell on such things at the
moment.

Yes, she decided, lifting her chin defiantly as
she reached into the cupboard and extracted
one of the gowns. Not only could she enjoy his
affections for a while, she would be remiss if she
did not. Besides, she had to think of poor Simmons. How crushed the maid would be if she
thought all her hard work had gone for naught.
Oh, yes, there was time and enough to set Lord
Edward straight; time to point out that he had
believed himself in love with another pretty face.

She refused to consider whether what she was
planning to do was wrong, pushing all feelings
of guilt firmly to the back of her mind as she
laid the gown on the bed and reached for the
buttons at her neckline. After all, who had time

for lying in bed contemplating a future without Lord Edward in it when she could be better employed trying on her new gowns ... and seeing if she could also create the magic Simmons did with the paints and combs ... and planning for her next meeting with Lord Edward ... and deciding how she might best lure him into some secluded corner and— What was that? A noise had come from the darkened corner of the room; a sound much like a deep, contented sigh.

Emily hastily rebuttoned her nightgown and snatched up her bedside candle, wondering whether to investigate or merely make a run for it. Holding the candle higher as she swallowed down on the lump in her throat and took up the heavy silver candle snuffer, she took a single tentative step toward the corner, unwilling to summon help, only to find that a mouse was playing in the baseboards.

"Good evening, darling," came a voice from the darkness. "Going somewhere?"

"Who is ... ? *Edward?* Is that you? Good Lord! What ... what are you doing here ... here, in my bedroom?"

The rough sound of a match being struck against a boot sole was followed by an illuminating flare of flame as Lord Edward touched the fire to the end of his cigarillo and took several deep puffs. "I think that should be obvious, Emily, my dearest. I am sitting here watching you sleep. Or at least I was, but you have awakened now, haven't you? I repeat, are you contemplating going somewhere at this late hour? I had heard you had the headache. Do you think it is wise to go out into the night air in your condition?"

While Lord Edward was talking, Emily, never taking her eyes from him, put down the candle snuffer and searched a hand restlessly over the bedspread, hunting for her dressing gown, which she hastily slipped on after placing the candle on her bedside table. She gave a moment's thought to blowing out the candle, thereby plunging the entire room into darkness so that Lord Edward couldn't see her, but discarded the idea, not liking being unable to see precisely where he was. She decided instead to take refuge in haughtiness, even if she failed to understand how anyone could be effectively haughty when dressed in a worn dressing gown, her hair done up in a braid, and sporting bare feet.

"You are being facetious, sir," she pointed out coldly, her chin at an arrogant tilt, "and upon further consideration I have realized that any explanation you might offer would be totally unacceptable. Please, just leave now, and we shall say no more about this temporary aberration of yours."

Lord Edward allowed himself to look crestfallen. "Ah, but, darling, that would totally defeat the purpose of my visit," he objected, pushing at the lock of blond hair that had fallen down over his forehead.

Emily had tightened the sash of her dressing

gown three times in as many minutes, flushing as she remembered that she had succeeded in opening all of the buttons on her nightgown before Lord Edward had bothered to alert her to his presence. Why, another moment or two and she would have ... But, no, she couldn't dwell on that now. "And just what is the purpose of your visit?" she heard herself asking after having already told him she wasn't interested in his motives. Really, this being alone in a boudoir with a gentleman was most unnerving; she didn't see how those opera dancers managed it.

"Do you really want to know? I'm not sure I should tell you. After all, I thought you weren't interested," Lord Edward answered promptly, setting her teeth on edge.

"I lied," Emily shot back, doing her best not to pick up the candle snuffer and brain him with it. "Now, tell me, and then leave. My aunt and cousin will be home soon, if they aren't already."

Lord Edward sat back in the chair and crossed his legs at the knees. "Yes, I know. When I left them with Del and Monty they were already discussing making an early evening of it. The theater was a crushing bore—you were right to give it a miss."

"How did you get in here?" Emily asked, this random thought hitting her a bit late, but not too late for her to be curious about his method of entry. "Surely all the doors were locked?"

"The windows too," Lord Edward agreed, his arms now folded across his chest. "Dare I tell you that Burton—who is the best of good fellows, by the by—has been so brilliant as to procure a key to the dowager's front door? Prodigious resourceful, Burton is, my darling. You'll like his way with a saddle of lamb, too, once we're settled in at Lyndhurst Hall."

The beast of a man was enjoying himself to the point of becoming obnoxious. "I'm not going to Lyndhurst Hall with you, Lord Edward. I wouldn't cross the street with you! And I detest saddle of lamb!" Emily knew she was being drawn into a ridiculous, immature round of brangling with him, but she seemed powerless to stop herself short of going on: "So there!"

Lord Edward picked up his cigarillo, which he had laid in the empty candy dish on Emily's dressing table a minute earlier, noticed that it had gone out, shook his head at it, and then replaced it in the dish. "I never did like the silly things, to tell the truth, but I felt the need to have something to do with my hands for a moment there when you were . . . But, no, I shouldn't be so frank, should I? What were you saying, darling?"

Hating herself, Emily repeated through clenched teeth, "I detest saddle of lamb!"

"No matter," Lord Edward assured her, tilting his head as he smiled at her most benevolently. "Wouldn't you be more cozy sitting down, my love? You look deuced uncomfortable standing there, holding yourself together. I didn't see anything, you know—or at least not much of anything. Not that I didn't try, you understand. You looked most fetching in that thin gown, with the light of a candle shining behind you. But we are engaged, so it really doesn't matter what I saw, does it?"

"We are *not* engaged!" Emily exploded, near tears. "How are we ever going to make anyone believe we don't want to marry if you persist in reminding everybody every second moment that we are betrothed?"

Rising from his seat, taking care to make no sudden moves so that Emily wouldn't run from him, Lord Edward walked slowly across the room, ending by standing three feet away from her, looking deeply into her eyes. "We are engaged, Emily. You're wearing my ring, remember?"

"I'm losing my mind," Emily remarked to no one in particular. "That's it. My grip on reality is slipping. I've been spending too much time with Aunt Hortense and Georgy, and now Lord Lyndhurst, and my mind has snapped under the strain. They'll be coming for me soon, to take me to Bedlam in a strait waistcoat, where I shall most probably spend the remainder of my miserable life explaining to everyone who will listen that I am not about to give birth to seventeen babies. I don't know why I didn't think of it before, as it explains everything. The rest of the world is just fine. This idiot standing in front of me right now, grinning like a painted doll, is totally lucid. No one is insane. *Except me!*"

"You're babbling, darling," Lord Edward pointed out needlessly as he rested his hands lightly on her shoulders. "Don't you think it's about time you stop fighting the inevitable and simply give in?"

Emily's wandering thoughts quickly returned to the matter at hand. "You mean, why don't I *marry* you? But that's ridiculous. You don't want to marry me; you never wanted to marry me. It was Georgy you were after, don't you remember? And it was Aunt Hortense who inserted that silly notice in the paper. We're only pretending to be engaged to protect ourselves from gossip. That was the way it was—I mean, the way it is—isn't it? But then your brother came . . . and you kissed me . . . and then you told me you . . . Oh, I don't know what I mean. I'm so tired, so confused."

Lord Edward's left hand slipped lightly across her shoulder so that his fingers could play in the braid that lay there. "I know it isn't polite to correct my own *fiancée*, but I fear I must point out that I did propose to you—*before* the dowager so much as picked up her poison pen. You turned me down flat, as I recall, saying you wouldn't have me if I were served up to you on a platter, or some such rot. I don't mind telling you, darling, I was crushed."

Emily tilted her head slightly, trying to disengage her hair from his grasp without being obvious. His closeness was doing strange things to her insides and she wished she could find some way to keep her teeth from chattering. "Now you're being completely ridiculous, sir. You never meant a word of that so-called proposal—you were only being hateful, as you always are with me. I didn't take you seriously for a moment, which you knew full well I wouldn't."

"And here I thought you were a smart puss," he chided, shaking his head.

Emily allowed exasperation to reign. "Oh, shut—"

There were several ways open to Lord Edward to prove that he had been sincere, to explain that he had wanted to marry Emily from the first, but he decided to take the most personally satisfying way, tilting up her head and claiming her mouth with his own.

He doesn't play fair, Emily screamed silently, trying her best to resist his charms. He either teases me or kisses me, and either way I . . . "Oh, Edward," she moaned against his lips, her arms going up to encircle his neck, knowing that if he was the winner in this latest battle she certainly wouldn't call herself the loser.

Kissing Emily was wonderful, but kisses such as the ones they were sharing could not continue indefinitely without Lord Edward completely losing control of himself, and he knew it, acknowledging their delicate situation by slowly, reluctantly ending their embrace and holding her away from him at arm's length. "Now," he said once he regained his breath, "are there any more questions, my darling Doubting Thomasina?"

Had she been given a few minutes to reflect in private and to recover from her beloved's gentle assault on her senses, Emily could have come up with a half-dozen questions, all very valid, but at the moment she could think of nothing to say except to babble: "You only think you love me because of my new gowns and the things Simmons did to my face and to my hair. Actually, Mr. Roberto did the things to my hair, to be perfectly honest, but you know what I mean. I think you should know that. I mean, it's only fair of me to tell you that, underneath it all, I'm still—"

Throwing back his head to laugh out loud, Lord Edward pulled her against him, hugging her in delight. "Underneath it all, my darling, you are the most wonderful, exotic, intoxicating creature nature ever made. Where do you come up with such nonsense? And only imagine, I was first attracted to you because of your level head. Apply to Burton, my darling, if you have any more misgivings, please, but I refuse to enter into an argument with you over whether or not I love you."

Emily burrowed her head against the front of his coat, embarrassed down to the tips of her toes. "Then . . . then you weren't dazzled by my new appearance?"

"I've always thought you were the most beautiful woman in the world. You've just stopped hiding it, thank heaven," Lord Edward assured her, whispering the words into her ear so that shivers of delight skipped down her spine.

"And you always wanted to marry me?"

"I always wanted to marry you."

"From the very first?"

"From the very first. You just refused to pay attention," he chided her, gently nuzzling her cheek with his nose. Hallelujah! At last he felt he was making some headway!

Emily shook her head, tears welling up in her eyes. "I still can't believe it. I mean, you certainly weren't nice to me, were you? No, I don't believe it, much as I'd like to. You were compromised by Aunt Hortense's announcement, just as I was. I think I should go back home to Surrey tomorrow, and then, in a few months, if you're still of the same mind, you can ... Oh, dear! That was the front door, wasn't it? Aunt Hortense and Georgy must be home." Pushing away from him, Emily grabbed Lord Edward by one hand and pulled him along behind to her door that led out into the corridor, laying her ear against the panel.

"Emily, you lovable, hardheaded nodcock, what are you doing?"

"I hear male voices too! Lord Henry and Lord Delbert must have come inside with them. You came in the front door, you said? How shall you ever slip past them without anyone seeing you? Oh, Edward, you clunch, you've done it again! How will we ever explain this away without

Aunt Hortense demanding that we marry at once?"

Lord Edward reached out his free hand and pulled open the door as Emily gave out a quiet squeal of protest. "I haven't the faintest idea, my demented darling. What do you say we trip off downstairs right now and ask her?"

Emily felt the bare floor on her feet as she was half-dragged, half-pulled into the corridor, one hand firmly stuck in Lord Edward's, the other holding on to the doorjamb for dear life. "Are you out of your mind?" she whispered hoarsely, her slanted eyes nearly round with horror. "I'm not dressed!"

"My goodness gracious. So you aren't," Lord Edward answered jovially, giving her arm another tug.

"You release my hand at once!" she ordered, her voice low and full of indignation.

"You want me to go downstairs and ask that everyone come tripping upstairs to reconvene in your bedchamber?" he queried, grinning—to Emily's mind—like a jackanapes. "Del might not mind, but Monty . . . well, I think his gentle sensibilities might be slightly overturned, don't you? But if you insist—"

"You come back here at once!" Emily commanded as Lord Edward started off jauntily toward the staircase, her voice rising in volume in spite of herself.

"Emily? Is that you?"

"*Georgy!*" she exclaimed, skewering Lord Edward with her eyes. "Now you've done it! They'll all be up here in less than a minute. You had better hope you really love me, Lord Edward Laurence, for you'll have no choice now but to marry me!"

And Lord Edward Laurence, feeling more than tolerably pleased with himself, relaxed against the wall, his hands folded across his chest, and smiled at his exasperated beloved. "Yes," he announced quite happily, "I will, won't I? And unless I miss my guess, we'll be bracketed within the week. Imagine that, my darling Miss Emily Howland. Finally I stumbled on a plan that worked!"

Epilogue

Lord Edward rode his new hunter across the lush green fields of Lyndhurst on his way back from the village, where he had been supervising the rethatching of three cottages. He reined in the horse atop a slight hill and pulled out his watch, checking the hour yet again, happy to find that it was almost time for luncheon and he could head back to Lyndhurst Hall, as he was sure his wife would be ready to leave within the hour. Turning his mount and urging him into a canter, he made for the carriage drive, planning to cut across its bottom edge on his way to the stables.

He was almost to the stable path when he spied two coaches barreling into the drive. Hauling on his mount's reins even as he gave out with an impassioned curse, Edward remembered his careless invitation to have his friends back down to Lyndhurst Hall for a house party a few weeks after the wedding ceremony that had taken place the first day of June in the family chapel with his brother and Emily's family looking on, just as the dowager duchess had decreed.

At the time, it had seemed a reasonable idea, having Lords Henry and Delbert down to Sussex to bear him company, as he had always found the country to be most boring in the past, but now he took the time to wish his two good friends on the other side of the earth.

"Yo! Ned! Don't look so glum. We're here to save you from the doldrums!" Lord Delbert shouted from the open window as the first carriage flashed past, leaving Lord Edward to rein in his nervous mount by the side of the road as a mantle of dust settled around his shoulders.

"*Yoo-hoo!*" Lady Georgiana trilled, waving a white lace handkerchief out the window of the second coach as it too passed in front of him. "Isn't this jolly?"

"Oh, God, not Georgy too!" Edward groaned, pasting a false smile on his face for Lady Georgiana's benefit. "If the dowager is inside that coach, Emily will murder me!" Digging his heels into his mount's side, he raced to the front entrance in the hope he could succeed in turning his friends back the way they had come before Emily came downstairs to discover them encamped in her house.

"Oh, isn't this just lovely, having us all together again?" Lady Georgiana exclaimed while standing in the middle of the foyer, dressed in a flattering rose-pink traveling ensemble, pulling off her long kid gloves as Lord Edward, slightly breathless, bounded through the open doorway.

"Hello, there, *cousin*," she said pointedly, happy to be able to claim the dashing lord as a relative, even if it was only by marriage.

"Lady Georgiana," Lord Edward choked back at her, seeing his two friends in the process of handing their hats and capes to one of the underfootmen. "I hadn't expected you ... er ..." He faltered as the young woman began to pout. "... so soon! Yes, that's it. I hadn't expected you *so soon*. I did, of course, expect you. Really, I did."

"You're babbling, Ned," Lord Henry pointed out as he examined his reflection in a nearby mirror, carefully arranging the top of his hair over that one nagging bald spot. "It seems we haven't arrived here a moment too soon."

Lady Georgiana noticed that Lord Edward was still looking at all of them rather strangely, and decided an explanation might be in order. "Lord Henry was visiting at Del's—you know he lives almost on top of us, of course ... Del, that is—and the two of them came over to see us last night—we had such a lovely visit, even if Peregrine did behave badly at having extra men at table, just as if he had the feeding of them, Mama says—and then Del said—or was it Lord Henry? I misremember—that we could make the drive to Lyndhurst in just above two hours, and that Lord Edward—I mean, Cousin Edward —had already invited them to share his boredom. Oh, dear, I shouldn't have said that, should I, even if Emily isn't down yet? Anyway, we decided, what with there being nothing to do at home, with dearest Mama down with the tooth-ache again, why shouldn't we just ride on over, because my maid could serve as chaperone until I was back with Emily, who is used to being in charge of me anyway, isn't she, even if she is Lady Edward now—imagine, I used to be bear-led by the wife of the heir to this whole estate, isn't it boggling!—and then Emily could take charge of me, because she is a married lady now, and so ... well ... here we are! Is that adorable Burton here? He's so little, isn't he?"

"Ain't she amazin'? She did that all with only two breaths. I tell you, Monty, I can't under-stand why I didn't see it before. Georgy's a most unusual female."

Lord Henry turned to look at his friend, won-dering if the fellow had hit his head harder the other day than first was thought when he top-pled from the dowager's dogcart. "Del, the girl's got less learning in her brainbox than a half-dozen gape-mouthed goldfish," he informed Lord Delbert quietly, not wishing Lady Georgiana to overhear him, for, after all, it wasn't her fault if she was a fool, was it?

"No one has goldfish for brains, Monty," Del whispered back repressively, believing his words had properly defended Lady Georgiana, then walked over to confront his host. "Ned, what are we doing cooling our heels here in your hallway? Not that it ain't nice enough, what with that really outstanding suit of armor propped over there in the corner and all, but we've seen it before, when we were here for the wedding.

Are you just going to keep us standing here knee-deep in Georgy's luggage? You know, anybody would think you didn't want us."

"Not want you?" came an amused female voice from halfway up the wide staircase, and immediately all heads turned in that direction. "Now, where would you get a silly notion like that, Lord Delbert? Lord Henry, darling Georgy, how wonderful it is to see you!"

Emily floated down the remainder of the stairs, her smoky blue muslin morning gown held carefully above her ankles, as the other persons in the foyer were turned for a time to marble, then swept across the tile floor to slip her hand familiarly through her husband's arm. "Edward, dearest, shall we show our guests into the main saloon?"

"I . . . I . . . er . . ." Edward replied brilliantly, Emily's bright smile rendering him almost speechless.

"Emmy?" Lady Georgiana squeaked, once she found her voice, her glorious emerald eyes open very wide as she quite pointedly stared at her cousin's magnificent bosom. "Is that . . . is that *you?* You look even more beautiful now than before."

Lord Delbert, who had only moments ago believed himself to be on the verge of tumbling into love with Lady Georgiana, nearly tripped over that young woman in his haste to reach Emily's side. "Please, Lady Edward, allow me to assist you," he pleaded, already extracting her from her husband's side to lead her toward the main saloon. "Ned shouldn't allow you to stand around like this, a female as delicate, as lovely as you. After all, you might take a draft."

That she might, Edward thought jealously as he watched his wife allow herself to be led away from him without a backward glance. Strutting around all but naked, that's what she's doing, he decided—forgetting she had worn that same gown only a week earlier and he had admired it greatly the whole time he was taking it from her in the privacy of their bedchamber—and he longed for nothing more than a large scarf which he could then stuff into the neckline of her gown.

"Gad, but she grows more lovely every day! I should have my pens, some paper. She deserves a sonnet, at the least."

"Monty?" Lord Edward prompted nastily as his friend, his face oddly pale, stood with his back against the far wall, staring after Emily's departing back. "I take it you are still impressed with my wife's new wardrobe."

"My God, Ned, I don't believe it!" Lord Henry exclaimed at last, slowly shaking his head. "She has turned into a goddess, a veritable goddess. I could see the beginnings of it in London before your marriage, but the transformation is total now. That face—so exotic! And that body—so ... er ... That is, how did I not know? How could I not notice—me, a poet! I'm supposed to see beyond the obvious. Ned, you lucky dog, you."

Lord Edward took his devastated friend by the elbow and led him into the main saloon,

which left Lady Georgiana to either pout by
herself in the foyer or follow on her own as best
she could, a very lowering experience for a young
woman used to being the center of attention.

Upon entering the room, Lady Georgiana saw
that both Lord Henry and her childhood friend
Del were sitting on low stools at Emily's feet,
looking up at her with the most sickeningly adoring looks on their faces. The young woman's full
bottom lip pushed itself forward a quarter-inch
just as her rounded chin began to wobble. Her
beautiful emerald eyes, the ones Lord Delbert
had told her reminded him of the color of
Scottish streams in full spate—his lordship being
quite the avid angler—filled with self-pitying
tears. She didn't like this, she didn't like this at
all.

She had come to bear her cousin company in
her unhappiness, for she was sure that being
compromised—not once, but twice—into marriage couldn't be looked upon as a happy event,
no matter how well Emily had pretended to
bear up under the strain. Witness her sister Henrietta, for pity's sake! But Emily wasn't the same
anymore. She had done something to herself, to
her hair, her face. Lady Georgiana already had
seen that in London, but the change seemed ten
times more noticeable now. She was almost
pretty. Emily wasn't *beautiful*, Lady Georgiana
comforted herself, because beautiful meant being
blond—with great big round eyes and pink-and-
white skin—and being *small*, and delicately made,
and . . .

"Lady Georgiana? Wouldn't you care to sit down?"

Blinking her big round emerald eyes several times to disperse the tears that she refused to allow to spill over, Lady Georgiana tore her gaze away from her unnatural cousin and looked up into his eyes. "Thank you, Cousin Edward," she gushed coquettishly, extending her hand so that he took it in his. "I thought everyone had forgotten me."

"What ho? We have visitors? Noddy, why didn't you have Burton come fetch me? I was in the nursery playing with the toy soldiers Father gave me when I was six. They'll need painting, Noddy, before your son can play with them. I think you chewed them in your cot, if I remember correctly. I've started with the red, you understand. I've always been partial to red. Hello, hello, everyone!"

Lord Edward turned to see his brother standing in the doorway—his clothing covered with dust so that it was obvious he had also been crawling around in the attics again, his fingertips covered with red paint. The marquess looked good for all that, having actually gained some weight since Emily had taken a hand with the menus, and with another—hopefully lifelong, once Lord Edward and Emily produced a child or two—"project" to keep him happy. "Reggie," he said, depositing Lady Georgiana into a chair, "you remember everybody, don't you?"

"Of course I do," the marquess assured him, shaking Lord Delbert's hand, and leaving that man staring at the paint smudges that were left behind on his palm. "But, Noddy, I thought you and dearest Dulcinea were leaving this afternoon. The Lake District in the height of summer. Delightful! I once spent two months walking there—or was that two weeks? But what does that matter? You'll adore it! I don't understand. You are still leaving, aren't you?"

"Leaving?" Lord Henry cried, looking up at Emily in desolation, wondering if his plans for a series of sonnets would come to nothing without the presence of his Inspiration during the creation process. "You're going away?"

"Leaving?" Lord Delbert repeated, looking over at Lady Georgiana as if belatedly remembering her presence, wondering whether the love of his life would ever find it in her heart to forgive him for this momentary desertion. "That may be for the best."

"Leaving!" Lady Georgiana chortled, turning to Lord Edward, her green eyes alight with sudden joy, believing that she just might be able to stand it if Emily disappeared out of her life for a while—if only until she had Lord Delbert's ring firmly on her finger. "How perfectly wonderful!"

"Leaving," Lord Edward concluded, winking at his wife, knowing that she was enjoying this little scene as much as he, and wasn't really angry with him after all. "Directly after luncheon, as a matter of fact. You are invited to dine with us, of course, and once we are gone, my brother can bear you company."

Burton announced luncheon, and the marquess,

struck just then with another brilliant idea, herded the three bemused guests into the dining room, talking nineteen to the dozen about the lovely painting party they would all have in the nursery—just as long as he was allowed all the soldiers with red coats!

"You invited them here, of course," Emily said sweetly as Lord Edward helped her to her feet, holding both her hands in his.

"For my sins, yes," he agreed, pulling her completely into his arms. "I was a bachelor much longer than I've been a husband, and I foolishly thought country life would still bore me to flinders. You know that's all it was, don't you, darling? I mean, you aren't going to go back to believing I really don't wish to be married to you?"

Emily lifted her head from his shoulder and smiled up into his adoring eyes. "Any misgivings I may have harbored have been well and truly disproved by these last few weeks, my love," she assured him, too happy to be embarrassed by her own boldness. "Did you notice? Lord Henry and Lord Delbert seem to think I'm pretty. Even prettier than you said I was in London that last week before our wedding. I think marriage must agree with me. Are you jealous?"

"Of course I'm not jealous," her husband denied, pressing his lips against her temple. "Now, let's go get this luncheon over with so that we may leave. I'm dying to be alone with you, wife!"

"First, give me a kiss," Emily demanded, pouting prettily. "After all, my darling husband, I have been very good, not teasing you for inviting the world here to share our honeymoon. As a matter of fact, I should be thanking you for not inviting them, and dearest Reggie, of course, along on our tour of the Lake District."

Putting a finger beneath her chin, Lord Edward raised Emily's face toward his. "I'll kiss you, minx, but first you'll have to promise me something."

"Anything," Emily breathed fervently, her gaze concentrating on his mouth.

"Promise me you'll send a maid upstairs for a shawl before we join everybody at table."

Emily's eyes twinkled as she laughed aloud, flushed with pleasure, for she was still very much enjoying her newfound attractiveness. "Ned! And you told me you weren't jealous!"

As he lowered his head to hers, Lord Edward whispered huskily, "I lied."